CANBYVILLE

When Sheriff Harris Bolton went back to the place where the bear had killed the old man and attacked his granddaughter, one thing was abundantly clear—it was one hell of a bear. Bolton's brother Jess volunteered to help him track it down, so they took a pack animal and an old buffalo rifle, and headed into the mountains. Two people had estimated that bear at three thousand pounds and as tall as a saddlehorse at the shoulder. Neither of the Bolton brothers believed that. But they hadn't met the grizzly then.

CANBYVILLE

Harry Foster

A Lythway Book

CHIVERS PRESS
BATH

First published in Great Britain 1980
by
Robert Hale Limited
This Large Print edition published by
Chivers Press
by arrangement with
Robert Hale Limited
1986

ISBN 0 7451 0376 6

British Library Cataloguing in Publication Data

Foster, Harry, *1916—*
    Canbyville.—Large print ed.
    —(A Lythway book)
    I. Title
    813'.54[F]   PS3566.A34

    ISBN 0–7451–0376–6

CANBYVILLE

CHAPTER ONE

HARRIS

The wind of autumn was sharp and gusty. Leaves dappled the plankwalks and eddied in untidy pools making sounds as dry as old corn husks. Earlier in the morning one of those great Vs of migrating geese had flown over, a mile long to each line, their lonely honking faintly heard in Canbyville.

Harris pulled a bone chip button through the loop of his rider's coat, sucked his head down deeper inside the collar and stood watching the arrival of the late-day stage up from Doringham. Those men on the high-seat looked numb. Each had a muffler over the top of his hat to keep the thing from being blown away, and wore gauntlets made of smoke-tanned elk hide, lined with rabbit fur.

The horses were roughening with winter hair and between whorls of wild wind their breath hung in the air like diluted smoke.

Harris shoved his hands into coat pockets and waited until the stage had turned up into its corralyard. His brother strolled up and stopped to watch also. They were alike in many ways. They were also different. Jess said, 'Harris, if he isn't on this one we might as well quit lying.'

1

There was no response until Harris removed his right hand from a pocket, unconsciously lifted and re-settled the holstered Colt, then started away as he said, 'He'll be on it. Go on back and stay with the folks.'

They were big-boned, solid men, thick in the neck, chest and shoulders. Harris was the least garrulous of the two and Jess was three years younger. His eyes were pale blue and his hair was as black as midnight. Harris's eyes were like those of his mother, very dark brown. He also had that coarse, thick, jet-black hair. People who could not possibly know such a thing for a fact said the Bolton brothers had Indian blood.

Around Canbyville such a thing was not exactly rare. The town was in the middle of the old Blackfeet-Sioux territory. It was a common joke that none of the oldtime buffler hunters had ever frozen to death ·in their bedrobes during Montana's early-dark long cold winters. If a man had charm he shared it. They would say that, then laugh.

The stager standing stiff as a ramrod besides his empty coach in the corralyard pulling off grey, lined gloves also had that stalwart, strong build and the black hair and eyes. He eyed Harris, whose badge was beneath the buttoned coat, and spoke through stiff lips without inflection.

'Yeah. We picked him up at Doringham, Harris. The way we knew him was the little

2

black satchel lyin' beside him on the plankwalk. Drunker'n a damned lord.' The stager jerked his head. 'I guess the cold revived him. He headed for the saloon before I'd set the brake. If you want the son of a bitch sober you better get over there.'

Harris turned without a word. One of those dust-carrying gusts of icy wind caught him at the corralyard gate without so much as making him brace in his hurried stride.

The saloon was a popular place even in mid-afternoon on this kind of a day. Generally though the rangemen and townsmen who congregated there only bought a drink out of courtesy. What they really wanted was to back up to the big cast-iron stove.

John Southwick, who owned the place, saw Harris Bolton shoulder in and because they had been friends for ten years John could read the marshal's expression correctly. John continued to idly polish a shot glass as he perceptibly jerked his head sidewards to indicate the thick-set, grey man of average height, nursing a glass of pale whisky.

At times it saved conversation if Harris unbuttoned his coat, which he did now as he stepped up beside the shorter, thicker and older man at the bar. 'If you're Doctor Ray, mister, we don't have a lot of time.'

The older man turned yeasty eyes, planted his feet solidly down and reached to enclose the shot glass in one hand. 'Sheriff, all the devils in hell could not move me out of my tracks this minute, until I'm fortified against the cold. And, Sheriff, I don't know why you people ever took this country from the Indians!'

The older man raised the glass with aggravating slowness, tilted his head and dropped the slug straight down, only swallowing once. Doctor Walter Ray was a man who knew how to drink whisky.

Harris Bolton reached for the bottle, nodded to John and when Southwick walked down, Harris handed over the bottle. Then he fished for a silver coin and dropped that atop the bar and turned. There was no mistaking the look on his face.

Doctor Ray paused just beyond the saloon doorway to roll up his collar and pull his curly-brimmed little derby hat lower. Then he gave a shudder.

'Where is he, Sheriff?'

Harris led off. 'It's not a he, Doctor, it's a she—eleven years old.'

Walter Ray was surprised. 'I thought that stager said it was a man—an old man.'

'No Doctor. The old man was killed. He don't need you. We got him over in the icehouse if you want to look at him later on. His granddaughter is the one that needs you.'

Doctor Ray's plump cheeks reddened with the chill. 'Before I examine her I'd like to know

4

exactly what happened,' he said, stretching a little to keep up.

'Her grandpaw took her for a buggy-ride into the foothills north of town. Yesterday was her birthday. The old man used to have a cabin back up there. In the early days. He trapped and hunted all the way eastward to the Wind River range. He loved the mountains and she loved her grandpaw. He used to hire a rig and take her up there in the summertime; teach her to fish and hunt a little.'

'Sheriff . . . !'

'Yeah. Well, that's their background, anyway, and how they happened to be up there yesterday. The rest of it we didn't learn until last night when she came around. It was a bear. Big son of a bitch. She said ten feet tall but she's little and a bear rearin' up above a little kid would look ten feet tall. The old man told her to run for the buggy. He figured to lure the bear away. And I guess he did. But a bear is faster on his feet than folks believe. He broke the old man like a tree limb, chewed hell out of him and when the little girl was screamin' at what she saw happening, the son of a bitch came after her. He got her too, but she was hangin' on to the buggy when the horse bolted. She hung on until she reached the road, then fainted, I guess. Anyway, the rig came back to town, folks started back, and meanwhile some rangemen from west of the road found her and brought her

5

in.'

Doctor Ray's breath steamed as he walked briskly along. Fresh, cold air was an excellent tonic, evidently. When they reached the clapboard house on the back street behind Mulligan's forge and Harris halted, Doctor Ray's blue eyes were clear and enquiring. He stepped over someone's discarded buggy tyre to the porch and put down his satchel to rub stiff hands together.

The woman who opened the door to them was tall and lean, man-built and man-shaped with auburn hair, grey-streaked, held severely back in a bun. She looked at the two men, said nothing and stepped aside.

The small parlour was warm. Too warm in fact for men who had walked briskly in the outside cold. Harris held his hat as he said, 'This is the doctor, Eleanor. Doctor Ray. Doctor, this is the little girl's mother, Eleanor Farnham.'

Doctor Ray looked right through Eleanor Farnham as he brusquely nodded. 'Where is the child?'

Eleanor turned. The house was small. It had a number of rooms and they were also small. Whoever had built the place had had an idea in his head and resolution in his heart, but no experience at all. Still, that over-sized wood-stove in the parlour was a blessing on days like this one. Its heat penetrated even to the back

6

kitchen and the storage shed which was attached to the kitchen by an afterthought-runway.

The little bedroom was cramped. A single bed, a battered dresser and a chair nearly filled it. Harris Bolton seemed out of place. His head was mere inches from the smoke-tanned ceiling.

The girl was lanky like her mother, but with large, soft eyes and freckles across the saddle of a tipped nose.

She was white to the hairline, moved only her eyes, and when Doctor Ray put aside the satchel, removed his derby hat and leaned, lips pursed, eyes narrowed to begin his examination the silent child turned big eyes to her mother and Harris squeezed aside so the woman could get next to the cot.

Eleanor talked softly and gently, giving reassurances which her daughter did not seem to entirely believe. The child weakly rolled her head. Harris met her haunted gaze—and winked slowly, then smiled.

Doctor Ray was thorough. He also smelled of whisky which was embarrassing to Harris who knew Eleanor Farnham's husband had died an alcoholic after fifteen years of shoeing horses and drinking steadily.

Outside, a gust of wind rattled loose roof-shakes and an unlatched door. The wood-stove made a chugging sound, once, as wind jumped down the stovepipe. A little grey dirty smoke escaped around the iron door, then the smoke

7

returned to the chimney pipe.

CHAPTER TWO

AN IDEA

The first thing Harris Bolton did at the jailhouse office was poke wood into the cooling stove. The second thing he did was rummage for the bottle in a low desk drawer and set it up for the doctor, then he shed his hat and coat, sank down at the desk and fished for his tobacco sack and papers.

The doctor took two swallows and went over to back up to the stove as he said, 'The buttocks will heal nicely. Excepting her wedding night, someday, who would see them anyway? They'll have bad scars. There's nothing to be done about that . . . Her back and shoulders will have to be stitched, Sheriff. But that torn tendon above her ankle...' Doctor Ray shifted position as heat began radiating outward at his back. 'They can't be ligatured you know. The chances are about fifty-fifty that she'll have a limp. In any event she can't use that leg for a long time; those tendons heal only when they are immobile. And it takes time. Not as much for her as it would for someone our age, but I believe after looking at her that the difference would be that where you and I could accept

8

sitting down a lot, and not doing anything, she's going to suffer almost as much from the inactivity as from the rest of it.'

Harris trickled smoke and got comfortable. 'Anything else?'

'Yes. Seeing someone disembowelled by an animal would sicken you or me. But we've seen similar things before. She's what—nine?'

'Eleven. Eleven yesterday.'

'Yes. Eleven, and she's never seen anything like that before. And it was her grandfather. Long after the body has healed, Sheriff, there will be terrifying dreams, periods of bad depression, and I'd guess fear of the mountains—but mostly fear of bears all her life ... Tell me about her father. She's going to require understanding companionship.'

'Her father died three years ago. He was the blacksmith's helper here in town. That house in fact belongs to the smith; he keeps it for his hired man ... Her father drank himself to death.'

Doctor Ray watched bluish smoke rise into the hushed air of the office above Harris Bolton's head. The jailhouse office seemed almost air-tight. Outside, the wind was coming steadily now, high as the rooftops. Inside, excepting for that soughing sound over the ridgepole and around the eaves, there was silence.

Doctor Ray rallied from unpleasant thoughts.

9

'When does the night stage leave?' he asked.

'It left about an hour ago, Doctor. We got a fair boardinghouse at the upper end of town. The morning coach heads south to Doringham right after breakfast. Usually about six o'clock.'

Dispassionately the medical practitioner said, 'Gawddammit.' Then loosened with resignation. 'Well, I can get something to eat at the saloon.'

'At the cafe across the road,' stated Harris, leaning to stub out his smoke. 'How big was that bear; you got any idea after lookin' at the old feller in the ice-house?'

'Do you want a guess?'

'Yeah.'

'I'll base it upon the power of the strikes and the thickness of the claws which tore through the old man. Now it's just a guess remember, Sheriff ... Well over a ton.' Doctor Ray watched Harris Bolton for reaction. When the tawny eyes came up, Walter Ray also said, 'I used to hunt a lot, Sheriff. I've killed two grizzlies in my time. Years ago, of course, when there were more of them around. Both of them weighed over a thousand pounds and they were not exceptional critters. This bear was a grizzlies ... I'll stake my life on it. And he was huge; probably old as well ... If you haven't had any reports of him before this attack, believe me you will have. They stake out a territory where they can find plenty of meat—grubs, deer, elk—

horses and cattle.'

'And old men,' said Harris, who had heard about grizzly bears all his life.

'Your local ranchers will hear about him if he's too old for fat does and elk yearlings.' Doctor Ray palmed a large gold watch, studied the fragile black hands, snapped the face closed with finality and pocketed the watch. 'It's past my feeding time, Sheriff.'

Harris arose and went to the door with Walter Ray. As they passed he said, 'Doctor, could you look in on her again in the morning before you leave?'

Ray nodded. 'Of course. I'll leave some goose-grease salve and some carbolic acid mixture. And I'll impress upon her mother again about the importance of keeping her immobile. Absolutely still on that cot for at least two weeks. Sheriff, you can help. Check on her every day or two.' Doctor Ray smoothed the front of his waistcoat. 'I'll be back in a couple of days. We'll sew her up a little then. When it's unlikely more swelling will tear the stitches.'

'I'm obliged, Doctor.'

Ray looked up from the dark plankwalk. 'There is something else to be discussed.'

Harris nodded. 'I'll see to it you get paid.'

Ray turned to depart. 'Thank you, Mister Bolton.'

The wind was still coming steadily at ridgepole-level directly from the icy north.

Harris closed his office door and went to briefly stand by the stove before taking down his blackened old coffeepot and filling it with water, then dropping in a handful of ground beans. He had no more than settled the pot atop the stove than Jess walked in, bringing cold in with him.

He pulled off heavy gloves as he studied the sheriff. 'What'd he say? I just saw him headin' for the saloon.'

'She'll heal in most places. But she got a torn hamstring and if it don't heal right she'll walk with a limp. He's coming back in a couple of days to sew on her back a little.'

Jess loosened his thick blanketcoat. 'What about the bear?'

Harris was reluctant but he said, 'He looked at the claw and tooth marks and how the old man was torn and slashed . . . Better'n a ton of him, Jess.'

The younger man did not show disbelief. He simply said, 'A grizzly then. It's been a long time since anyone's seen one around here, Harris.'

The coffee began to give off a pleasant scent as Harris went back to his desk. Jess reached for the bottle Doctor Ray had left, took a couple of swallows and handed it over. Harris returned it to the lower drawer. He sat down gazing up at his powerfully built younger brother. 'Remember that old man named Showalter who lived in a shack behind the boardinghouse?'

12

Jess sat down and pushed back his hat. 'He's been dead five years. Old bear hunter.'

'I sure wish to hell he was still around, Jess. Aside from him and Cindy's grandpaw there's no one left who hunted grizzlies.'

Jess thought a moment. 'Maybe on the reservation there'd still be some old broncos who'd know how to get at this one.'

Harris continued to thoughtfully gaze at his brother. 'They wouldn't do it.'

'They might. If they knew this one tried to kill a little girl.' Jess shoved out thick, oaken legs and studied the scuffed toes of his boots. 'I can ride up and talk to them.' He lifted his glance. 'You want to go after the son of a bitch, Harris? I'll get us a pack animal in case we got to stay out a few days.'

The sheriff smiled. They had not always got along during their growing years, but they had lately, and of all the men Harris knew, if it came down to a choice of companions in an affair of this kind, he would select Jess. He said, 'You got your cows to look after at the ranch.'

'Yeah. And you got this town and the Saturday night drunks ... Harris, give that critter a little time and he'll be eating off me, calves and colts to start with, then cows and horses. Me and the other stockmen. I was over talkin' to John at the saloon. There's just one thing that's got to be done and puttin' it off until all the cowmen are up in arms won't help,

13

because by then we might get an early snow.'

Jess paused. He was by nature a direct, forthright individual. Too blunt at times. He was also a hard worker, a hard drinker, when he drank, and a man who lived hard every day of his life. As powerful as oak and clear-headed. To some people he was abrasive. He was to his brother at times, too. Harris was less likely to speak out, more inclined to think and keep most of it to himself. But physically they were identical; powerful, large men, quick and solid.

'All right. If you want to, ride up to the reservation. When'll you get back?'

'Couple of days.' Jess yawned, then said, 'I don't trust that damned sky. I know it's early but I've seen early snows before. Deep ones. If it'd clear up maybe we could count on three, four days up there in the mountains.' He stood up and re-set his hat, pulled out his gloves and pulled them on. 'Over a ton? That's hard to believe, Harris.'

'You've heard of them that large.'

'Yeah. When we were kids. And I didn't believe it then, either. But I'd sure like to see one that big. It'd settle it in my mind that they really grew that big.'

'I hope you don't see this one standin' up, Jess.'

After his brother departed Sheriff Bolton got his cup of black coffee. The wind was gusting again, the temperature was dropping, and out in

14

the road a couple of rangeriders loped southward talking back and forth about an early snow storm.

Jess was right, of course. If they didn't kill that grizzly soon the drifts would be too deep for a horse to plough through them. The rest of it was basic; no huge, heavy bear would remain up where snowbanks were half as high as he was, where he'd sink to his belly with every step. He'd come down into the lower country, perhaps to the alder-thickets of the foothills and live off tame livestock. Or maybe people, although that was not much of a possibility. Even if he killed another person he probably would not eat the meat. Tales of man-eaters were not rare. Like his brother, Harris had heard of man-eaters, and even as a youngster had suspected that was just tall talk. He was still confident it was tall talk. This particular grizzly had made no attempt to eat the old man, just kill him and scatter him over a couple of acres.

He returned to the roadway where the cold wind of early evening had become an icy discomfort now that nightfall had arrived. There would be a rind of frost on the vegetable patches by morning and stockmen would have to use bootheels to bust through ice for the stock to drink at water-troughs.

Tim Ellis, the harnessmaker, came out of his shop and turned to lock up as Harris Bolton came along. Tim looked up and smiled. 'Early

15

winter,' he called, and Harris paused to say, 'Every winter's an early one. I'm never ready for 'em.'

Tim agreed with that. 'Damned cold gets into a man's bones. Specially the joints.'

They parted near the tie-rack out front of Southwick's place where a pair of bundled stockmen reined in and came down to the ground a trifle stiffly. The stockier of the two flashed a wide smile at Harris and called through the wind. 'Come on inside. I'll stand the first round. I got something to tell you.'

This night, even though it was the middle of the week, John Southwick's saloon was noisy, smoky and warm despite all the draughty doors and windows, and cracks in the outer as well as inner plank siding. That old cannon heater was popping. Every few minutes someone went over and shoved in a piece of wood. The women and kids were snugly at home around kitchen or parlour stoves, but at John's place the townsmen and rangemen congregated in a totally masculine atmosphere and John's bar was thriving. He grinned at the two rangemen with Harris Bolton, produced a bottle with three little glasses then hustled elsewhere.

The stocky cowman shoved thick gloves into his pockets, loosened the rider's jacket at the throat, shoved back his hat and turned a cold-reddened face toward the sheriff as he poured. 'My riders killed an old boar bear this morning, then back-tracked him into a thicket and found the sow. They'd been eatin' a big yearling heifer.' The cowman lifted his glass, tipped his head and downed the whisky neat. His companion, a taller, leaner man, did likewise but Harris let his glass stand while he waited, then said, 'Two of 'em, Paul?'

'Yeah. The sow wasn't very old but the boar had some teeth missing. He was mangy and old. Too old to bring down anything but cattle and colts . . . Drink it down, Harris. This is a hell of a cold night.'

Harris drank it down then placed a big palm over the little glass, so the cowman turned and re-filled his companion's glass, then his own.

Harris said, 'How big was the boar bear?'

The cowman looked at his lanky companion. 'Fred . . . ?'

In the act of raising his re-filled glass the second cowman paused to say, 'Six hundred. Maybe six hundred and fifty pounds.' Then downed his whisky before speaking again. 'I was bringin' in some horses when I heard the gunfire and headed over there. Spencer and Tracy, couple other fellers who work for Mister Jordan, had the boar down and was finishin' him off. He was still willin' to fight even after they broke his back. Then the three of us back-tracked him to where the sow bear was, in an alder thicket eatin' on the big yearling.' The lanky man grinned. 'That old bitch had a lot of fight in her,

17

for a fact. She scattered us like quail until someone's shot busted a shoulder and she went down. But we had to tie the horses and go back on foot to finish it.'

Paul Jordan listened as though he had not heard all this three or four times before, during the day out at his ranch. He shook his head at Harris. 'We went back with a wagon to skin her—his hide wasn't worth it—cut off their heads and take 'em back to the ranch. By gawd, Harris, that's the first bear-attack on my range in six or eight years. And it'll be the last . . . I don't think she'd have come down that low if the old boar hadn't. Hell, he was as old as a man.'

Harris said, 'What kind of bears, Paul?'

The cowman's answer was curt. 'Black as Toby's butt. There's cinnamon bears in the mountains but they don't come down. Anyway, they're never big enough to do much damage. But black bears . . .' Paul Jordan wagged his head. 'If we hadn't got that pair, Harris, they'd have raised Cain among the cattle and horses this winter before they went and denned up. And come next spring they'd have come out hungry to start a real killin' spree. Care for another jolt?'

'No thanks.'

'I'll have her hide tanned and boil meat off the heads for the dogs.'

Harris said, 'Yeah.'

18

Fred leaned around his employer to say, 'They must've ganged up on that yearling. She out-weighed both of 'em, and it must have been a hell of a battle because by gawd she was strung out over more'n an acre of ground, hide, meat, guts and all. And those tracks was big, Harris.'

'The bear tracks?'

'Yeah. Of course it rained last week so slidin' and lungin' like they had to do made the tracks look a lot bigger, but when he had a chance to look around after we killed her, it was enough to make a man's hair stand up.'

Harris gazed steadily at Fred for a long time, until John came along to see if they needed anything, then departed while Paul Jordan filled his own glass again and shoved the bottle over to his rangeboss. As Fred reached to also pour again he said, 'We been thinnin' 'em out on this side of the mountains for years now. I haven't seen bear sign in a hell of a long time. I figure these bears must have maybe summered up along the rims on this side, and when the cold came they drifted down lower on our side.'

Paul Jordan nodded his head throughout this statement. The red in his face which had been produced by being exposed to the freezing weather on the ride to town was being replaced by a different shade of red. In a voice which seemed to have more drag and slur to it now he said, 'We're goin' to make a sweep of the foothill country in the next few days. Just in case there's

19

more bears up. I'll be damned if I want 'em fattenin' up on me before they burrow in for the winter. I never did like bears. Bears, wolves, cougars, but mostly bears... Fred, let's go down to the cafe.'

Harris returned to the roadway with them and after they had hiked southward through the cold wind he stepped to the lee of Southwick's doorway to roll and light a smoke. Afterwards he arrived at a decision which did not make him particularly happy; he would ride up into the foothills in the morning—if it wasn't snowing, but he doubted that it would be.

CHAPTER THREE

A DAY OF SUNSHINE

In the morning the sky was bell-clear and the sun was shining, which surprised everyone after that lowering fish-belly sky of the night before.

There was thin heat in the sunlight but visibility was perfect. It was possible to make out each wide-spaced individual tree up along the mountain top-out northward when Harris walked from his place at the boardinghouse down to the liverybarn where he kept two horses. One was a stout, sagacious sorrel. The other was a seal-brown ridgling who would fight

20

geldings and tease mares. Everyone including the liveryman either disliked the seal-brown, or else they knew what he was from sight and reproved the sheriff for keeping him. But for brains, bottom and downright truculence, the things which made a horse as tough as a boiled owl, that pig-eyed, thick-jawed, stud-necked seal-brown ridgling had no match in the Canbyville countryside. He could not be turned into a corralful of other horses; he had to be stalled and close handled, and watched like a hawk because, while he would not kick, he would certainly bite. It cost Harris an extra two dollars a month to get the liveryman to keep him at all.

That was the horse he meant to ride this morning. But as he was passing the stage office he encountered Doctor Ray looking mean and rank, so reaching the barn to rig out had to be postponed. The doctor buttonholed Harris with a fierce look and said, 'They sent out the damned morning coach an hour early. Just like that. Without so much as posting notice on the front of the office, or saying anything. I came down to buy my passage and by gawd the stage was gone. And that 'possum-bellied agent in there just shook his head at me.'

Harris understood. Stage schedules were never more than generalisations, which was why it was called the 'morning' or 'evening' stage. He attempted an explanation with some thought

21

in mind of being placating.

'We don't have much call to be very exact in Canbyville, Doctor. And usually they haul out mail or light freight more than passengers, so they send 'em along when they're loaded—sometime after sunup. I'm sure sorry.'

Doctor Ray was not to be placated. 'Sorry? Sheriff, I have a cellar full of sorries. I have a practice to look after down at Doringham.'

Harris looked southward, down to the front of the liverybarn as he said, 'Ask around town. Maybe someone's got a rig going south today.' He smiled at Doctor Ray. 'I wish there was something I could do. Right now, I got to ride out; it'll be a long ride and I got to get going.'

He stepped around Walter Ray, striding southward. The doctor gazed after him, flintily, then ranged his gaze elsewhere, swore with feeling and stepped down into the wind-swept roadway heading for the cafe. And that was another thing about this damned town: the saloon did not open until high noon.

The liveryman was up at the cafe and his dayman was reluctant to get the ridgling so Harris led the horse out to be tied and saddled. He lashed his coat behind the cantle. He and the seal-brown had long ago arrived at an understanding, and while neither of them was demonstrative, they liked each other. The horse had only bitten Harris once. For two days afterward he had had trouble eating. Once he

22

had tried to buck Harris off. Because he had come unwound without warning he had succeeded. But as soon as Harris could stand up, he climbed back astraddle, and that time the ridgling was set afire from flank to shoulder. He had never bucked again.

They rode out of town by the west-side alley under a dazzling sun across an open countryside with frosted grass crackling underfoot, heading northwest up across Paul Jordan's range. The air was chilly but there was no wind, which was a blessing. Harris could tolerate all the phases of weather in Montana, but wind. He had been a rangeman for six years before applying for the job as township constable when the former constable died, so he had been accustomed to Montana weather in the Canbyville countryside long before he became the lawman. He also knew livestock. When he had first become constable it was a fact that he knew livestock better than he knew men. But that had changed; along with the sprinkling of grey over the ears, Harris had acquired an education. He now knew people as well as animals. By the time he was completely grey he would have wrestled many times with the matter of which he liked best. And by then he would know for a fact, which he trusted most.

He saw cattle off to the left a few miles. They were strung out grazing southward which told him they were probably the critters Paul's riders

23

had been pushing down away from the foothills yesterday when the men had encountered those bears.

That was a clue and he reined off accordingly. He had not asked where the riders had killed that pair of black bears.

Trailing over the sign left by the moving cattle was not difficult. These animals were greasy fat. They left droppings like stepping-stones for a mile above where Harris rode in behind him.

Another time buzzards and magpies would have led him to the carcasses. There were still magpies in the foothills but the buzzards had departed, and they would have led him directly to the bear remains with their high circling. Magpies clung closer to the ground.

But he saw them finally, flashes of brilliant black and white among the alders. They scolded him when he rode up toward the stand of alders, flapped and screamed and hopped along the ground with all the indignation of dispossessed owners, and he laughed at them.

Then he found where coyotes had been at work. From there it was a matter of another few yards to reach the carcass. The ridgling's nostrils flared, his little piggy eyes widened, and his steps became stiff and stilted, but he did not offer to whirl and run as another horse would have done. Still, when Harris halted to dismount the ridgling was relieved not to be made to go closer to the gory mound of hair and meat.

Harris did not go very close either, but for a different reason. She was indeed a black bear. Judging from the tufts of hair left behind by Jordan's skinners she had been sleek and not very old, but large and fat. The dead yearling heifer had added more meat and hair, reddish this time, to the trampled, discoloured grass in all directions. As Fred Baker the rangeboss had said, she had been a big yearling. Pound for pound she had been heavier than the sow bear, but muscle for muscle she had been no match at all.

Harris made a cigarette, smoked it pacing here and there studying tracks, signs of the battle, and finally walked beside the best set of tracks where a bear had gone back to the thicket after the kill. The stride was longer than his by more than a foot.

He killed his smoke, went back to step across leather and begin a quartering ride in search of the boar bear. There were shod-horse marks overlying bear tracks. It was as good to follow one as the other since the riders had come northeast after killing the old boar.

He found the boar finally, not through the tracks but by the feeling of the horse under him. His ridgling had piccked up the smell a mile before Harris saw the big, furry carcass, swollen like a flour-sack out in the open country. Harris too picked up the scent from a fair distance. That old boar had been living off carrion for a long time. He smelled worse than a tan-yard and the seal-brown would not go closer than a quarter mile. He simply dug in and stood like granite, willing to be hooked or even thumped on rather than take one more forward step.

There was nothing to tie him to so Harris stepped down bringing the Mormon hobbles with him. When he went ahead the horse was still standing like a stone facing the way of that sickening stench.

This time the tracks were more difficult to make out because the rangemen had raced around shooting, and afterwards had trampled the whole area on foot, but tracks were not necessary. The boar was lying on his side where he had died, stiff as a ramrod and badly bloated with each of his four feet off the ground. This time, too, when Harris rolled and lit a smoke it was not because he felt a need but because the smell of the bear called for some kind of defensive action.

The boar's feet were larger than the sow's feet had been, but they lacked a good six inches of being as long or as wide as those larger tracks back yonder where the yearling had been killed. Harris studied the carcass, trickled smoke and softly said, 'Rain, hell. No rain made these bears slide *that* much.'

He went back to the seal-brown, removed the

hobbles and snugged up the cincha while gazing out where the boar bear was lying. He was satisfied about a hunch which had occurred to him last night at the saloon. The black bears Paul Jordan's men had killed were indeed eating the yearling heifer, but sure as hell they had not killed her.

Those tracks Fred had said were longer and wider because of the sliding and lunging, were not the sign left by the dead bears. They were grizzly tracks, and that was what had tantalised Harris Bolton last night, and this morning.

He rode southward for a mile before the rough shake roofs of Jordan's place were in sight, slightly to the west. There was smoke rising in a pole corral behind the huge old massive log barn, and long before Harris could smell burning meat and hair he understood what that rising smoke portended. Paul and his crew were working cattle through their marking ground, taking care of the autumn branding and cutting.

It was a good day for that; cold but windless and sunbright.

He rode down into the yard and swung off at the tie-rack in front of the barn. The men had seen him approaching. Paul came walking up through the barn looking sweaty despite the cold, pulling off grimy gloves as he came out front to say, 'We got a fire out back if you want to get warm, Harris.'

The sheriff was not that cold. He had something on his mind which would in any case have made him prefer talking to Paul where there were not billows of choking smoke, bawling animals and loudly cursing men.

'I just looked over those bears,' he told Jordan, as the cowman came up and leaned upon the rack, looking unshaven and ruddy and faded.

Jordan nodded. 'We heard wolves up there last night. They had 'em scattered even more, didn't they?'

'Yeah. Pretty much. Paul, did you know an old man around town named Farnham?' At the blank expression on Jordan's face Harris said more. 'He was the father of that feller who used to shoe horses at the—'

'The feller who drank himself to death?'

'Yeah. He was that feller's paw.'

'No, I didn't know him, Harris.'

'Well; couple of days ago the old man took his granddaughter up into the foothills. They got attacked by a bear.'

'You don't say!'

'The bear killed the old man and darn near got the little girl, but she's mending. Maybe she'll end up with a limp but at least she's alive.'

Jordan leaned there shaking his head.

'Paul, the little girl described the bear. It was a grizzly.'

Paul's eyes raised slowly, sceptically. 'Come

on, Harris. I've been in this country all my life and I've never seen one. Neither have you. Yeah, there's always been talk around, but ... You look like you believe it.'

'I think she was right, Paul.'

'Aw hell, a little kid sees a black bear and he looked ten feet tall to her. And she was scairt half to death.'

Harris could deny none of it. That had been his initial reaction too. But he said, 'Go back up there and look at those tracks again. No slidin' or runnin' black bear could possibly make sign that big, Paul. Yeah I know; it rained last week. That's what your rangeboss said. But go back up there and look around where that critter came flat down and *didn't slide*. Then compare his sign with the feet on your black bears.'

Jordan continued to lean and regard the sheriff. Harris said no more. He knew what the reaction would have been if he had offered Doctor Ray's estimation of the grizzly. Outright disdain.

Finally the rancher spoke. 'Have you talked about this around town?'

'No.'

'Don't do it, Harris. If you do, every nitwit who owns a big-bore gun will be ridin' or drivin' all over my fall feed, and if they stay up there at night every time one of my bulls bellers they'll be trying sound-shots in the dark.' Jordan straightened up off the hitchrail. 'It's bad

29

enough this time of year without that. I get horn-hunters and pot-hunters every hunting season by the dozen. We patrol up there to run 'em off as best we can, and every damned year I lose a cow or two despite the patrolling.' Paul stood gazing steadily at Harris Bolton for a moment longer, then spoke again, but this time with a faint sound of anger or hostility in his voice.

'This hasn't been too good a year for cowmen, Harris. We've had a lot of poison weed and redwater. And now the market's down again. I got to trail out three hundred yearlings within the next few weeks, and the damned weather's beginning to look a little ugly too, like we might get an early winter and snow before we're ready for it. Harris, I don't need any more trouble. If you start yellin' grizzly they're goin' to come from a hunnert miles in every direction.'

Almost any reaction from Paul Jordan would have been expected by Sheriff Bolton but this one. He stood returning the cowman's gaze, unsure what to say so he said nothing. Then, finally, as Jordan fished out his gloves and pulled them on as though to signify they had said all they had to say, Harris tried one idea which had occurred to him on the ride down here.

'I'm not going to yell grizzly. I'm not going to say anything about this at all, Paul.'

Jordan's craggy features softened. He almost

smiled when he said, 'Good.'

'But I'm going after the son of a bitch. Jess and I, and if we can find one, an experienced bear hunter.'

Jordan finished with the gloves before answering. 'Harris, you and Jess and some damned bear hunter go trailing up through my range from town, you might just as well stand drinks at John's saloon and announce what you're up to.' Jordan stood a moment in thoughtful silence, then he said, 'Keep off my range, Harris. I'm not goin' to stand for any of this gawddamned foolishness. We're friends and we been friends a long time, but you're about to cause me trouble I don't have to stand for, an' I'm not goin' to tolerate it. You and Jess, and this other son of a bitch whoever he is, keep off my range, and gawddammit I mean every word of it!'

Paul Jordan turned in fiery anger and walked back down through his log barn leaving Sheriff Bolton looking after him.

CHAPTER FOUR

BY STARLIGHT

After Harris finished relating his experience out at the Jordan place his brother drily said, 'We're

31

not doin' so good, are we?'

Harris went over to stoke the stove. While his back was to Jess the younger man said, 'Three days ridin' and all I got was unfriendly looks from the young In'ians and a lot of talk about the spirit of returning grizzlies from the old ones. As soon as I left I bet you a new hat those old bucks gathered around and made medicine to the spirit.'

Harris was not surprised. 'You couldn't get one to come along?'

'No. But I got a lot of advice against going after this ghost of a great hero bear. Anything happen while I was gone?'

'No. Like I said, Paul's black bears didn't kill his red heifer, and he got mad when I told him we were goin' after the son of a bitch.' Harris returned to his chair. It was hot in the jailhouse office. The coffee they had been drinking did not ameliorate that condition, either.

Jess sat slouched, his coat open, his hat far back, his unshaven, cold-reddened cheeks flushed and shiny. He had not even stopped by the cafe after putting up his horse at the liverybarn, but had come directly to his brother's office.

It was evening with a clear sky outside and stars bright as diamond chips in the congealing temperature; there would be black frost by morning.

Jess methodically made a smoke and lighted

32

it, strong features slack as he reflected upon his three wasted days, and the fresh disappointment he had just encountered in conversation with his brother. He gazed at the popping stove and said, 'Paul's right about one thing. And sooner or later folks are going to hear the story of a big grizzly. They'll come from all over to hunt it down.' He swung his head a little. 'Now what, Harris?'

Since the morning before and his conversation with Paul at the ranch Harris had thought about little else, so he gave a short answer. 'We go after it. Or, if you can't make it, I'll go after it.'

Jess's features tightened perceptibly. 'What do you mean—if I can't make it? Why couldn't I? I got no wife, and I can hire a feller to fork feed for me for a few days. Or have you got something else in mind? Harris, I didn't ride my butt numb over this bear just to come back here and set by the fire. You got someone else to go after him with you?'

Harris smiled. 'No. And if there was someone, I'd rather have you along. I can't cuss at some damned stranger when he does something stupid.'

They regarded each other over a silent long moment before Jess finished his coffee, arose and put the cup on the edge of his brother's desk, then started to button up and rummage for his gloves. 'All right. When?'

'How's the weather look in the mountains?'

'Cold as a witch's tit but clear. It'll hold.' Jess roughly smiled. 'Those In'ians told me the weather'll hold for a couple of weeks. That means it could come a big snowstorm tomorrow. Naw; it looks good, and if that bear hasn't finished storing up fat for hibernation he's going to be doin' nothing but eating until he's got enough. You say when.'

'Day after tomorrow I'll be at your place in the dark. Jess, we're going to need a pack animal, plenty of grub—and you'd better take along paw's old buffler gun. A cannon would be better, but the buffler gun'll have to do. You got loads for it?'

'Yeah. Some anyway. How about a bear trap? I got three hangin' in the barn. Big and heavy as hell.'

Harris looked sceptical. 'If he weighs anywhere near what Cindy Farnham figures, and that medical man said, we don't have a trap in Montana that'd hold him. And all we want is a few good shots.'

'How about the hide? It's worth a month's pay.'

Harris arose smiling at his brother. 'Let's get him first. Then we'll think about the hide.' At the door with a hand on the latch he looked steadily at Jess. 'This son of a bitch will kill on sight. And he can pick up a scent a mile off.'

Jess appreciated the warning. 'So will I,' he

34

replied. 'Kill on sight.'

After his brother's departure Harris blew down the lamp mantle, set the stove damper so there would still be coals in the morning, locked the jailhouse and went up to Southwick's saloon where a scattering of customers were either at the bar or among the old tables near the stove playing poker or blackjack.

It was a quiet night, John reported. Only a few rangemen had ridden in. Mostly, the townsmen were staying at home tonight.

Harris had a reason for being at the bar, aside from his customary nightcap. He told John about the pair of black bears Jordan's riders had killed, then downed his whisky as Southwick said, 'Good. That'll take care of them for killin' Old Man Farnham. By the way, they got Farnham in a box to bury maybe tomorrow if the ground isn't too frozen. Miz' Farnham was at the general store yesterday and asked me if you'd be a pall-bearer. She'd been lookin' all over town for you, and asked me to ask you, if I saw you.'

Harris nodded and pushed the whisky bottle aside as he leaned in the pleasant heat. 'Yeah . . . Tomorrow?'

'They figure the ground'll be soft by mid-afternoon,' stated the saloonman. 'You wasn't figurin' on not being in town tomorrow, were you?'

'Yeah. Yeah, I'll be in town—tomorrow.'

'By the way, did you see that sawbones before he left?'

'Briefly, out front of the corralyard.'

'Well; he was mad. But he did something before he left. He couldn't get out of town until evening anyway, so he sewed up Farnham's little girl. Fixed her up good, so the blacksmith told me. You know, he sure didn't impress me as much of a doctor, but I guess he was.'

Harris was interested, and decided even though it was close to eight o'clock, a time when most folks would be readying for bed, he'd go down there and visit a little with Cindy and her mother. His excuse would be that he'd only just heard Eleanor Farnham wanted him to be a pall-bearer for her father-in-law.

The walk cleared his head of the lethargy created by too much heat at the saloon, and every step crunched, even in the dirt of the alleyway out behind the blacksmith's shop.

Eleanor Farnham stood in the doorway looking peculiarly blank-faced, as though a lifetime which had rarely been easy and this latest blow had left her unable to feel. Harris told her why he had come, to assure her he would be a pall-bearer, then stood holding his hat until she invited him into the parlour.

Her daughter was bundled on the sagging old sofa near the stove with very dark circles under her eyes and a drawn, exhausted expression down around her mouth.

Some cold came in with Harris Bolton, along with a very faint whisky-tobacco scent which was totally masculine and which was also foreign to this little house. His size too, created something different. He smiled and winked. The little girl's eyes kindled but she otherwise showed nothing as he went over and dropped to one knee beside the sofa.

'You hurt,' he said to her, 'and I hurt because you do. But you know, Cynthia, it all goes away with time. You're pretty. Life was made for pretty little girls, and if you'll do exactly as your maw says, when you're up and around again I'll take you buggy-riding over to Bee Spring and we'll have us a picnic.'

Eleanor left the room briefly and returned with a cup of hot weak coffee for Harris. He thanked her; she did not have a dime, those grounds had been boiled and re-boiled. He arose and stepped to a straight-backed oak chair as he tasted the coffee. He said, 'Good,' and watched Eleanor's expression undergo no change. 'You have plenty of wood?'

Eleanor barely nodded. 'Mister Waters from the blacksmith shop brought some over yesterday. Tag ends of lumber from an old cabin he's tearing down west of town on some property he bought last summer. It's dry as a bone.'

That subject was exhausted and Harris tasted the coffee again. He looked over at the child,

37

uncertain and groping. He had known her from babyhood. What the hell was a person supposed to say? He tried. 'You got a slate, Cindy? You're goin' to miss some school, but you know what? Lyin' around, by golly, you'll have time enough to maybe learn more this way than if you were at your desk.'

Eleanor's large, soft eyes showed appreciation when she spoke. 'That's right. I borrowed four books from school for her. Geography, history, arithmetic and spelling. I guess I'll learn right along with her, Sheriff.'

He sipped more coffee. Goose-grease salve was fine. It healed harness galls, saddle sores, and they even used it on fistulas. It also healed cuts and hurts on people but by gawd if it wasn't fresh, and it never was, in a too-hot room it had a bad rank odour.

Harris wished for a smoke but made no move to reach inside his coat, and when the silence had drawn out to its limit, the little girl spoke for the first time. 'Mister Bolton . . . ?'

'Yes'm,' he said, loosening all over and smiling again.

'I need . . . I need something. Mister Bolton.'

'You tell me what it is, Cindy, and by golly you'll have it.'

'I need . . . an uncle.'

He felt Eleanor's eyes misting as they turned to him but he did not look away from the little girl. 'You got one, Cynthia. You got one as long as you live. Can I be him for you?'

'Yes. I wanted you for him, Mister Bolton.'

'Well, by—golly—you quit callin' me Mister Bolton. Uncle Harris sounds better anyway.' He finished off the watery coffee to dissolve the lump and handed the cup back to Eleanor as their eyes met. Eleanor seemed almost as though she might smile, but she didn't. She did not show anything at all.

Shortly after this moment Cindy's dark-ringed eyes turned drowsy and Harris left. Eleanor stepped briefly outside with her holding an old shawl to her shoulders, lanky and mostly flat, but strangely handsome in the icy starshine as she said, 'It's so hard to talk, Mister Bolton. She doesn't ask about grandpaw, she lies there looking out the window, and I know she's got to talk it out.' The woman's large eyes lifted to Bolton's face. 'I guess I'm a coward. I don't want to start it. I'm frightened of what will happen when I do.'

He nodded, because that was easy to do, and she probably expected it of him, but also because he did not know what to tell her. He said, 'I'll be a pall-bearer tomorrow, but commencing the next day I'll be gone for a spell. My brother and I.'

Her lingering eyes neither wavered nor blinked but she took a breath before speaking. 'You're going back up there? You and your brother?'

'Look around a little,' he admitted, turning at the distant bark of a dog at the upper end of town.

'Has there been—anything else about the bear, Sheriff?'

'No ma'm.' He turned back towards her. 'My notion is to take care of it before something else happens.'

She clutched the shawl tighter and he smiled a little. 'Sure cold tonight isn't it? Good night, and don't let her use that leg.'

He walked back down the alley, conscious of her standing in the cold watching, then he angled over to the main thoroughfare and plodded noisily over ice crystals all the way up to the boardinghouse.

Before entering the old barracks-like building he paused in the roadway where he could look far northward where the mountains rose, a thick black bulwark dividing the Canbyville country from the upper country beyond, which was mostly timber, and huge meadows for cattlemen to trail into each late springtime, mostly uninhabited.

He looked up there and said, 'I owe you,' then he went up along the sagging porch and went inside where a single hanging lamp with a dirty glass mantle gave all the light there was along the plank-floored hallway leading to his room.

The boardinghouse always smelled of fried

meat. Even in the middle of the night. And this night it was still warm so evidently the big iron stove in the threadbare parlour had a deep bed of coals.

Dogs barked, the sound as clear as though they were almost beneath his window. Varmints were prowling, as usual, raccoons wrinkling their noses at the scent of chickens in their locked-up henhouses, skunks and badgers and other scavengers waddling among the buildings in search of trash-cans. The dogs rarely caught one, and when they did, if it happened to be a badger they'd get badly cut up. No dog could whip a badger. And if it was a skunk someone would put the dog on a long chain as far from the house as they could.

There was a scimitar-moon which Harris had noticed earlier, speculating upon spending a few nights in the mountains with no more light than that. But as he kicked out of his boots and rolled the holstered Colt in its shellbelt to be put atop the chair-seat at the bedside, he thought now about the little girl who would someday grow into a tall, handsome woman like her mother had been, once, before the weight of life had crushed and mangled her emotions.

Hell, a little limp wouldn't detract from a beautiful girl. As for the scars, well, luckily she had been running when the bear had made his swipe and all the marks would be in the back. As that whisky-drinking doctor had said, no one would notice them until . . .

Harris yawned, scratched hard, and climbed between the cold cotton sheets.

CHAPTER FIVE

CRIPPEN

Fortunately they had put all that had been recovered of old Farnham in one of those waterproofed mail sacks used by the stage company, and it fitted neatly into a small square box, so digging the grave had not been excessively difficult; not after the grave-diggers had got past the first three inches anyway, and the sun was brilliant for the burial.

Harris stood on one side of Eleanor with Art Waters, the short, burly and oaken blacksmith, on the other side. Eleanor's face was covered by a black veil, which helped, but Harris could feel the spasms as they came and went while she stood erectly resolute, looking dead ahead across the far winter landscape while the Baptist preacher spoke.

Most of the town had turned out. The sunshine helped, otherwise all that endlessness of dead range grass, bare trees and cold would have made the ordeal much worse. Harris had stood like this, hat in hand, fresh stove-blacking on his boots, gun and shellbelt tactfully left atop the desk at the jailhouse, many times. He did not feel as sad now for the old man going into the ground as he felt for his daughter-in-law and his little granddaughter, but death made an impression. It always did. Part of his nature was pensively solemn anyway, so these affairs created a mood in him of silent, unsmiling gravity for hours afterwards.

It also bothered him that when they began shovelling in the dirt the damned ground was frozen into fist-sized boulders which rattled down upon the box with a terrible sound. He reached for Eleanor's gloved hand and tightly held it. Then he took her by the elbow and turned away to walk her home.

She moved automatically, did not say a word, did not see people and kept that odd, dead-ahead stare right up until he released her arm at the doorway of the little house. Then she lifted the veil and said, 'Thank you,' and went inside.

He went back to his office, shed his black coat, got his fleece-lined cowhide jumper, swung the shellbelt into place and buckled it with a savage jerk. There were several things to be done, so he went across to the general store, told the proprietor he might have to be gone for a day or two and weathered the inquisitive look he got, then bought some tobacco, a fresh box of slugs for his Winchester, and went up to Southwick's saloon.

There were three old gaffers playing pinochle at a shadowy table on the far side of the crackling stove. It was too early for customers. John was reading a St Louis newspaper two weeks old by peering alternately over the top of some glasses mid-way down his nose, or squinting directly through the lenses.

He put the paper aside, carefully folded his spectacles, placed them on the backbar then turned with a look of interest. 'How'd she make out? I was back in the crowd but she looked all right from there.'

Harris leaned, thumbed back his hat and fixed John with his tawny stare. 'Sometimes I wonder what in the hell folks got to have all that gawddamned hardship in one lifetime for.'

John's answer was short. 'Don't look at me.'

'Well; there's something I want you to do, John.'

'Sure.'

'The jailhouse is empty so no one's going to have to mind it very much.'

Southwick blinked, but kept quiet.

'And those black bears I told you about Paul's men killing?'

'Yeah. What about them?'

'Did you tell anyone?'

'Well,' stated the barman, beginning to look a little uncomfortable. 'Around a bar men talk a lot and that's about all some of them wanted to discuss ... Yeah, I told them Paul's riders had settled the score for the old man . . . I shouldn't have?'

'That's why I told you, John. So it would get around. That's what I want you to do for me. Keep on tellin' folks about those black bears and how Paul's riders got even for the old man.'

Southwick frowned faintly. 'That's not much of a favour to ask, Harris.' The frown deepened. 'What the hell is this all about?'

Harris ignored the question. 'For the next few days sort of look in on Eleanor Farnham and her kid, will you?'

'Yes . . . You sound like someone going out to be shot.'

Harris smiled. 'Set me up a glass and bottle.'

John complied. He set up two glasses. He rarely drank, and almost never this time of day, but something was wrong; he could feel it in the marrow of his bones. He filled both glasses and looked straight at Harris Bolton, then lifted his glass without speaking and downed the whisky. His eyes watered, and he made a weak joke.

'I'm sure glad I don't have to pay to drink this stuff.'

Harris talked about the weather. He also discussed the Farnhams, but this time he was concerned about their meagre woodpile, and John Southwick's uneasiness kept increasing until just before the sheriff departed. He said, 'Harris, you're up to something. It's likely none of my damned business—but all the same it worries me.'

The sheriff laughed, offered to pay and when John swore about that, the sheriff winked and walked out of the saloon into the slanting rays of a lifeless sun hovering above the shiny peaks of the highest icefields to the northwest. Cold again tonight; well hell, from now it wouldn't be anything else until next summer.

He ate like a bull elk at the cafe and with darkness prematurely arriving he got his booted Winchester, stuffed his coat pockets at the office, then went down the back-alley so people wouldn't see him packing a saddle-gun on his shoulder.

The liveryman had gone home. His nighthawk was an old man, stringy as a length of cured jerky, who kept bottles cached around the barn and overhead in the hayloft. His name was Abner. If he had a real name no one used it and Harris did not know it. The old man's eyes were brimming with water which was not occasioned from the cold when Harris walked in from out back carrying his Winchester.

Abner moved with jerky, almost spasmodic, movements. He jumped up from his tilted-back chair and stared, less at Harris and more at the loosely-carried carbine. 'You want a horse?' he asked. 'Sheriff, it's a hell of a night to be ridin' out. Goin' to freeze a man to his saddle afore sunup.'

'The ridgling,' Harris said, and propped the

booted weapon outside the harness room as Abner went jerking away for the horse. He had the saddle, the saddle blanket and bridle balanced against his thigh when Abner returned stepping along in an almost tiptoed walk, watching the horse from the corner of his eye. He cross-tied him instead of single-tying. Abner had never been bitten but he knew the ridgling would bite and he was very prudent around him. Everyone was, except Harris who stood waiting for Abner to finish cuffing the horse, then he rigged him out with Abner standing to one side fidgeting.

The horse was docile, but his malevolent little eyes did not leave Abner. He knew better than most horses did, when he had someone buffaloed.

Horsemen out in the roadway made a dry, rattling sound as they came down through town. It sounded like three or four of them and curiosity made Harris lean across the saddle-seat to watch when they passed the barn's wide front opening. They did not pass, they turned in. There were four of them and five horses, one being led on the turks-head end of a lariat. The others obscured that led horse as they entered the barn, filling the runway when they swung off without a word even though they had seen and recognised Sheriff Bolton.

One man, average except for his white hair and bold, lined face, stepped ahead leaving his reins dangling as he strode forward where Harris was standing. 'Thought I might have to roust you out of bed,' he said, and gestured with a gloved hand behind him. 'I got a dead man here, Harris.'

The other riders had lowered the poncho-wrapped bundle to the earthen runway. Abner scooted around to look, but Harris had a bad premonition and continued to lean across his saddle-seat. 'What happened, Mister Shaw?'

'I don't know. I'm not sure. He was a young feller came in last spring to ride for the season. His name was Tom Crippen and that's all I know. Except that he was good with horses and never loafed on me.' Shaw half turned to glance back where his other riders were standing beside the bundle wrapped in soiled old bedding canvas. 'I paid him off this morning and he rode out to find his personal horse this afternoon and never come back. We went out after supper, figurin' he might have got bucked off or maybe fell in the rocks or something.' Shaw drew a breath and faced Harris again. 'Whatever got him ... maybe a hell of a stout cougar ... busted his neck with one swipe; damned near tore his head off. Then clawed hell out of him and busted his back until when we went to pick him up it was like liftin' a sack of rocks. He bent every which way.'

'Cougar?' said Harris, walking around the rear of the ridgling.

A stooped, wiry and grey old rider snorted. 'Naw. Bear, Sheriff.' He stooped to pull back the old tarp. 'No cougar could do *that*.'

Tom Crippen's head was lying inside his right armpit but still connected by frothy flesh to the stump above the shoulders. His clothing was soaked in frozen scarlet and one leg was completely reversed, the toe down, the heel up.

Harris heard breath rattle in old Abner's throat. The nighthawk spun away and disappeared in the darkness beyond the sooty light of a solitary hanging runway lamp.

The rangemen stood like statues until Harris leaned and flung the canvas back over the body and straightened up to say, 'This afternoon?'

Shaw answered gruffly. 'That's what I told you.'

'How fresh?' asked Harris.

The older rider said, 'Damned fresh. When we found him the blood had set up but it was still sticky. It wasn't froze nor anything like that. We figured maybe he'd been attacked a couple hours before. Just about at sundown, maybe. Maybe even a little earlier.'

Harris turned toward the rancher. 'Where? In the foothills?'

Shaw answered cryptically. 'No. About two miles south of the foothills. Out in the open where the horses had been. But they sure as hell wasn't there when we arrived. And the Good Lord knows where they got scattered to by now.

49

If it was a cougar he was likely stalkin' the horses. I got about eleven, twelve head of late colts runnin' with the other horses.'

A young rangeman leaned and held out his hand toward Harris. In it was a sixgun, butt-foremost. The cowboy did not open his mouth but that old rider did. 'Ain't been fired. Ain't even been cocked, Sheriff. Whatever got Tom come up onto him too fast for him to do anything. Maybe just come up out of the tall grass.'

Harris examined the fully loaded gun and handed it back. 'Trees out there,' he asked, 'or some big stands of brush?'

'Both,' replied Shaw, rummaging in a pocket for his plug and worrying off a cud which he pouched into a leathery cheek. 'Mostly brush.'

'Tracks, Mister Shaw?'

'I expect. But it was dark and we wasn't exactly prepared to look, after we found the lad, Sheriff. In the morning we're goin' back up there, though.' Shaw chewed, turned aside to expectorate and turned back. 'We'll find the son of a bitch, and when we do we'll weight him down for all time. That was a good young feller. My wife and me liked him right from the start. This played hell with her. She's always been too damned motherly. You know that, Harris.'

The ridgling shifted stance, his saddle rubbed leather over leather and Harris said, 'All right. You want to bury him at the ranch, Mister

Shaw?'

'Yes. Maw says beside our boy on the little hill behind the house. You need any part of him, or any of his possessions?'

Harris shook his head. Then he said, 'Don't go back up there too early in the morning.'

Shaw understood the implication. 'We won't spoil the tracks. But we're goin' up there. Nothing's going to stop us.'

Harris nodded, went over to untie his horse and lead him out back before stepping up. His last sight of the rangemen in the sooty runway was when he turned northward up the back-alley, and glanced back.

He let out a big long breath of air while riding over freezing ground on his way up out of town. Jess's place was northeast too, but closer to the foothills than the Shaw place.

Beyond town he made a smoke. It did not give much comfort but it offered him an opportunity to do something with his hands, and that helped.

Privately, he had been half-hoping that grizzly bear had left the country after killing old man Farnham. He faced that thought now, but hoping instead that he had *not* left. Maybe it was natural for a man's feelings to be ambiguous about something he instinctively felt helpless toward. He had his sixgun and his saddlegun. He knew from bear hunts in the past that even a small black bear's sloping, massive skull would

51

turn a carbine slug like a wood splinter. And this was no black bear. His skull would be thicker, and if he had been able to catch that mounted cowboy—*on a damned horse*—he'd only been able to do it by somehow or other concealing his scent, and that was the most frightening thing Harris contemplated as he rode northeasterly in the direction of the foothills.

The ghost of a hero grizzly?

Damned dumb Indians anyway. His grandfather had been one, but he had died before Harris or Jess had been born. There were stories, though, and Harris remembered most of them about the old man. His mother had said her father had been a mystic; a genuine medicine man. Keeper of some sacred bundles.

Harris stubbed the smoke out atop his saddlehorn and hurled it away. How did that son of a bitch get that close to a horse? To a man, at dusk when the man wasn't expecting anything at all like a grizzly attack, it was understandable. But a *horse?*

Some wolves sat back and sounded to the thickening little scimitar-moon from a far mountainside. Maybe five, maybe eight miles distant and it sounded as though they were in the lodgepoles just behind his brother's place.

Harris was a solidly practical man. So was Jess. They felt two ways about their Indian heritage, but the way life worked out for most men like they were, there was no time, and not much inclination, to think about things of that nature. It took all a man's time just to keep a little money in his pants and beans under his belt—or behind it anyway.

CHAPTER SIX

AN EXCHANGE OF IDEAS

Jess held the lantern high until his brother had turned the off-saddled horse into a corral and forked some feed to him, then Jess yawned, shuddered from the biting cold and led the way indoors where he set the lantern atop a table and went to stoke the stove.

He ignored his brother until he had poured more water into the coffeepot and set it atop the stove. Then he turned and said, 'It's the middle of the night. I thought you weren't comin' out until morning.'

Harris was shrugging out of his coat when he answered. 'I wasn't, but then I figured we could get an earlier start if I was out here.' He tossed the coat aside and pulled a chair around to straddle it, gazing at Jess. 'Have you run across a young feller named Crippen who rode for Shaw?'

'Sure. Lots of times. He was the only one of

53

Shaw's men who knew how to break a horse. They never bucked with him. He never let them. Nice feller. What about him?'

'They brought him to town this evenin' busted all to hell. With his head about torn off. He looked like ground meat.'

Jess regarded his brother in the unsteady, sooty lantern light. 'What happened?'

'He went north in the direction of the foothills looking for his horse.' Harris tossed his hat atop the table and scratched. 'Shaw's got an old rider working for him. Shaw said it was a cougar. The old rider said it was a bear. Jess, what I can't figure out was how that bear got up that close to Crippen while he was on a horse.'

Jess methodically removed two cups from wall-nails and placed them on the table, then he sat down. 'Grizzly,' he said, making a statement rather than a question of it. 'How near to the foothills?'

'They said a couple of miles southward.'

Jess's gaze brightened. 'That's about where Shaw's range cuts over and meets my line.'

Harris was unsure so he said, 'Somewhere out there. We'll make a sashay and look around in the morning.'

'You're not goin' to be able to see much in the dark, Harris.'

That did not matter very much. The details were not that important and Harris wanted to be well away from open country, up into the brakes, before sunrise. He did not want to be visible before daylight.

'We can see enough,' he replied. 'Anyway, Crippen's dead and the important thing is the bear. We somehow got to be out of his range before he knows we're up there.'

Jess did not question his brother's deduction about the killer of Tom Crippen. He accepted the premise that it was the grizzly again. He pointed to a thick bedroll, some laden *alforjas* and the pack saddle near the door. There was a stubby-barrelled thick, ugly rifle over there too, old with scars on the dully oiled stock. 'I found nine bullets for the buffler gun,' he said, and kept gazing over there. 'It's a good thing the bufflers couldn't shoot back. It takes a long time to eject the casings from that thing to plug in a fresh load.' He fished in a pocket and set up a dull brass casing nearly as thick as a man's thumb atop the table. The slug itself was huge by almost any standards, and it was moulded lead. 'Soft lead,' he said, gazing at the big cartridge. 'It'll flatten on impact and make a hole where it comes out a man could drive a team of mules through.'

Harris knew the old gun. 'The range,' he said quietly. 'You got to be closer'n you have to be with a Winchester.' He was thinking of three thousand pounds of enraged bear charging. Then he switched the subject. 'You got the pack animal?'

55

'Yeah. And I got an old cuss from town to live here and look after things while we're gone.' Jess arose to fill their cups and return with them to the table. Now, he was wide awake but when his brother had ridden in he had been sleeping like a log. 'Harris, I got a feeling this is going to turn into something.'

The sheriff blew on his coffee before tasting it, and looked over the cup-rim at his brother. 'You superstitious about bears, Jess?'

The younger man reacted swiftly. 'Hell no. That's silly.' Jess let his cup sit there. 'Are you?'

Harris smiled a little. 'No. But . . . why did he attack Crippen, and it sticks in my mind about Crippen bein' on horseback when the grizzly got him. You never in your life saw a bear that didn't smell to high heaven, especially a boar bear.'

Jess looked annoyed. 'Aw, you're beginnin' to sound like those old buck In'ians I talked to on the reservation . . . Drink your coffee and let's get some sleep.'

The cabin was made of adzed, square logs joined at each corner with meticulous care. Jess was an exacting man about some things. There was only one room, but it was large, chinked solidly so no draughts got inside, and had three bunks on one wall. Jess, as lord of his domain, slept in the lowest bunk. Harris had to go up over the rungs at the foot of his brother's bed to reach his own bunk.

56

The last thing Jess did was stoke the stove with a dry burl to keep the place snug until morning. It made for good sleeping but when a man walked outside after arising the cold seemed ten degrees worse than it was, and they did not get much sleep because of Harris's idea that they had to get clear of open country before daylight.

Jess knew where things were, so Harris fried their breakfast by lamplight while his brother went out back and brought the pack animal around. He was adept at this sort of thing. He was also quiet. Like many loners Jess Bolton did not start the day out with a lot of talk. But he worked surely and efficiently. The only time he paused was when he secured the buffalo rifle between their bedrolls atop the pack. He threw the hitch over the waterproof canvas atop the load with the gunbarrel sticking out. He shoved it back and the butt stuck out at the other end. He shook his head, pulled it forward again and grumbled to himself with steam rising with each word in the dark, bitter cold.

He saddled his own horse and brought Harris's ridgling around, but looped the shank through a stud-ring on the side of the cabin out of kicking or biting distance of the other animals, and when he went inside beating his gloved hands together he said, 'When are you goin' to get rid of that damned stag?'

Harris answered curtly, 'Never. Eat up and

let's shag on out of here.'

Jess sat down with his blanketcoat buttoned to the throat, a red scarf wound around his throat and his old black hat pulled low. He removed the gloves but that was all, and he said, 'Every blessed winter I tell myself come springtime I'm goin' to sell out and go down south where it don't freeze every night after August.'

Harris said nothing. He ate, finished the hot coffee, took his plate and cup to the tub and left them in greasy lukewarm water. Then he made his first smoke of the day and went out to saddle the seal-brown.

The moon was a tad thicker than it had been but it was still a long way from being full. Stars shone with a cold white brilliance, more of them than a man could count in a lifetime. The purple heavens were flawless, which was reassuring. All the talk Harris had been listening to lately of an early winter and a big storm, seemed false this morning. There was not a cloud in sight.

Jess came out, closed the cabin door and pulled on gloves as he went over to free his horse and turn it a few times before stepping up. He leaned from the saddle, yanked loose the shank to the pack-animal and turned away, leading off around the cabin northward.

Every sound was magnified, every breath was a burst of steam, and every exposed square inch of flesh tingled with cold, but the northward mountains were ghostly, looming in the long hush of approaching winter, much closer in appearance than they were in fact.

Nothing was said for a full hour, then Harris diplomatically wondered aloud where Crippen had been attacked and his brother pointed with his rein-hand. He had given this considerable thought. He knew this range backwards and forwards, and while he had no idea where Crippen might have gone, he knew for a fact where the Shaw-ranch remuda hung out, so he rode toward that area.

He sashayed a little, until his bay horse abruptly changed leads with his head high, little ears nervously pointing, then Jess spoke without looking around. 'Bear scent—or blood scent.'

They had to hobble the horses with stiff fingers, take down their Winchesters and go ahead almost a mile on foot across stiffly frozen grass that crackled with each step they took, but they found something. Not Crippen's horse, but a big dead redback brockle-faced cow with a slack bag to indicate she had long ago weaned this year's calf.

Harris grounded his carbine looking at the disembowelled cow. She had been partially eaten. The rest of her had been dragged by small predators, carrion-eating wolves and coyotes. Her head was twisted over her back and it had been turned several times, probably by the impact of the blow which had downed her.

Harris said, 'I'll tell you what I think, Jess. I think Shaw's going to find this cow after daylight, then he's going to understand why his rider got attacked. He's got to be around here somewhere—the horse I mean. Crippen rode into the area where the grizzly was feedin' on this cow.'

'Why didn't he see the damned bear? It was daylight, wasn't it?'

'Shaw said Crippen went horse-hunting in the afternoon and they didn't find him until after nightfall. Maybe it was dusk.'

Jess went gingerly ahead avoiding frozen entrails and torn-off pieces of meat. He looked a long time at the carcass in the eerie starlight then he returned to report. 'She was older'n a man. Shaw must have missed her during culling time. Maybe she didn't see anything.'

Harris was sceptical. 'She still had a nose, Jess.'

'Well, the bear came onto her downwind.' Jess pointed to a stand of spindly jackpines. 'He could have waited over yonder until she grazed this close.'

The details in this instance did not really matter. Harris was satisfied they had arrived at one sound conclusion about this entire affair. Why the grizzly had attacked the mounted man. He led the way back to the uneasy, wary horses.

Jess quartered in the search for the place where Shaw's rangerider had been killed, but without much co-operation from his bay gelding. There was fading bear scent in the icy air, made sharper by the cold even though the scent was no longer fresh. Only the ridgling did not hang in the bit. Even so, he responded less to his rider than to his senses. He walked with a hump under the saddle, stiff-legged and with his little pig-eyes constantly moving.

The pack horse, a mare, was about as much afraid of the ridgling-scent as she was of the bear-scent, but the ridgling-scent was closer so she alternated between sucking away when Harris rode close, and flinging up her head at the bear-scent.

They found the mangled horse with the assistance of a foraging pack of coyotes. The noise of the little animals whirling away in sudden panic over frozen grass took Jess to the dead horse.

The saddle had been torn loose and hurled. The seating-leather was ripped off and the cantle had been crushed back, broken loose from the sills of the saddletree. It had been a good stock saddle with a bullhide covered tree. There was no way to crush that cantle without immense strength.

But the horse had not been eaten. At least not by the grizzly although other, lesser predators had been burrowing through into his soft parts.

This time Jess remained with the horses while Harris went ahead. When he came back, pulling off his gloves to roll a smoke, he said, 'Crushed like a damned grape, Jess. Picked up bodily and crushed, rib-bones, spine and all.' He waited until the cigarette was smoking before saying anything more. 'That bear. . .'

Jess nodded slightly. 'Yeah. Stronger'n an ox.'

'I told you what Cindy Farnham said, and what the doctor said.'

Jess handed over the ridgling's reins. 'I know what you told me. We got about two hours. Let's go.'

Harris smoked, moved with the easy rhythm of his mount and watched the distant mountains retreat tantalisingly as they rode toward them. They would be up there before sunrise, no question of that.

Jess turned once with a question. 'Eight hundred pound horse?'

'A thousand. Maybe eleven hundred. Big and stout. Young horse,' his brother replied.

A hundred yards farther along Jess spoke again. 'What is it they say—a man can lift just about his own weight. Maybe twice his weight if he's built for lifting?'

Harris stubbed out the cigarette. 'Damned if I know. Speakin' for myself, I weigh a tad over two hundred and I once lifted the rear end of a stone-boat full of boulders that they figured weighed nearly a thousand pounds. Maybe I lifted about four hundred pounds. But only a couple of inches off the ground. I won a bottle of whisky.'

Jess rode another short distance before speaking again. 'Did he crush that horse on the ground?'

Harris did not believe so. 'It looked to me like he lifted him into the air, Jess. Lifted him, crushed him while he was moving, and flung him down about four, five yards from where they first came together.'

Jess sighed, beat his gloved palms together and looked ahead as he quietly said, 'Maybe the little girl wasn't so far off at that. If the bear lifted and carried a thousand pound horse, he'd weigh maybe two thousand pounds.'

'Or three thousand,' Harris commented drily.

Jess stopped moving his hands. 'Gawddamn,' he muttered and did not speak again until they could begin to feel uneven ground underfoot in the cold darkness. When his brother came up to ride stirrup Jess said, 'I don't believe it.'

Harris had not believed it either, to start with, but he saw no value to keeping this discussion alive either, so he watched the foothills begin to break clear of the rearward darker heft of the vast cordillera. They were on the outskirts of the foothills with plenty of darkness left. If they chose to, they could get well up onto the first mountain-slope ahead of sunrise.

CHAPTER SEVEN

GARTH

When daylight arrived they had crossed up out of the alder-brakes and knobby little upthrusts of the broken country at the base of the meadowed and forested mountains.

Visibility improved but it remained cold even though the sun teetered like an enormous fireball upon the farthest rind of the curving earth, flooding the Canbyville range with newday brilliance.

They both knew this territory, Jess even better than his brother. Jess hunted up here every early autumn for his winter meat. Harris had hunted it, but not as extensively as his brother had.

Dark-barked fir trees as round and erect as totempoles stood in tiers upon the lift and drop of all the slopes. But there were also meadows scattered throughout the mountains, mostly unused except by the wapiti, deer, other grazing or browsing animals. Cowmen had long ago been discouraged from taking advantage of the stirrup-high feed up in here; there were simply too many native predators, and the angry sweeps made in years past by cowmen who had lost critters up in here had not seemed to lessen the number of meat-eating wild animals at all.

Trappers ranged the mountains, remnants of a host which a generation earlier had numbered thousands on foot and on horseback. Pot-hunters too, foraged for red meat to be sold in the towns and villages, but generally the high country had reverted in ownership to the animals which had originally been here.

Periodic posse-hunts had not perhaps diminished the wolf packs much, but they had certainly taught bears and wolves, cougars and other killers not to go too far off the mountainside because rangemen shot on sight and they were always armed when they skirted the area between the foothills and the cow country.

To Jess this was almost a private reserve. He pointed to a fir-topped rim and related in matter-of-fact tones how he had got his bed-robe up there when a black bear had come down at the smell of Jess's horse.

They went in a half mile then halted to blow the horses, and Harris went to a creek for water, studying the ground as he walked. He had a theory which had been fairly well authenticated by fact: the grizzly was staking out his territory and for some reason had chosen the foothill-mountainside area about a mile or so west. Perhaps bringing down that old redback cow had encouraged him to believe he had found a good territory for his needs. The second cow—

along with a man and a horse—had doubtless reinforced his conviction.

Harris tossed aside his hat, knelt and drank and was coming up to one knee when across in the mud among some blueberry thickets was something which caught and held his attention. A fresh footmark.

He stood up, re-settled his hat, jumped the creek and pushed in among the underbrush. There were more tracks, clearly made by a man and just as obviously not made very long ago. The tracks were heading northwest up away from the creek into tall timber and eternal gloom. On the way he conjectured. By the time he got over to his brother and explained about the boot-marks he thought he had an answer to their appearance up in here.

'Someone's ahead of us. Someone's heard about the grizzly and is after him.'

Jess frowned. 'On foot?'

There had been no horse-sign. 'If he's got an animal he must have left it somewhere, maybe in a meadow-camp.'

Jess continued to look sceptical. 'Alone? Well, he probably don't know what he's up against. See any other tracks?'

'None.'

They cinched up, heading northwesterly, not because the human tracks led in that direction but because after brief discussion they had decided to go up and around the grizzly's territory, then to make a base camp and hunt from there southward, easterly and westerly. Everyone was to some extent a strategist, and it helped if strategists knew their adversaries. Neither of the Bolton brothers had ever seen a grizzly bear, let alone acquired much knowledge about them. But they had both hunted black bears. There had to be some resemblance.

They became about as interested in the man-tracks always marching ahead as they were in watching trees for bear-sign, berry bushes, bee-logs when they encountered them occasionally, on the ground.

The grizzly had not been through here, or, if he had been, it must have been a long time ago, and he must not have been foraging. Harris guessed he had come through the high-country on an angling southerly course to the foothills. Jess grunted. He was not much of a theorist. He was looking for bear-sign or a bear. The rest of it he'd leave to those like his brother who might want to speculate.

The cold was less up in here, although perhaps because the sun rarely got through it should have been colder. The creeks still had rinds of ice along their backwater eddies, though, and most of the birds were gone, which Jess deplored; especially the scolding camp-robbers who sprang from tree to tree raucously scolding every intruder. There was no better way to plot the course of something than by listening to the birds. Now, there was an occasional flash of high movement but almost no noise at all.

The horses first detected a scent. Their riders passed along another hundred yards among stiff-topped rough-barked dark monarchs of the uplands before they also detected it. Smoke.

Harris halted, sat a moment getting his bearings in relation to the fragrance, then pointed in silence with a gloved hand and they rode onward.

Whoever he was, without doubt he had gone into an early camp, and that meant there was probably a meadow dead ahead.

Jess shook his head. No one in his right mind would be in this area on foot and alone.

Harris had an explanation. 'He hasn't seen bear-sign.'

They were riding single-file with smoke-fragrance guiding them along before they made out the little clearing where the game-trail split, one trail heading directly for the stirrup-high grass barely visible through the trees, the other half going cautiously up and around the clearing. Most of the big game animals up in here did not graze, they browsed. Grass to them was bedding, they did not live off it.

Harris halted, swung down pulling out the saddlegun as he reached the ground. Without speaking Jess did the same. They tied the horses and strode the final few yards to the edge of the clearing on foot.

There was no particular reason to be wary of another man up here but instinct made men that way. Ten miles from the nearest habitation in primaeval forest there was no law, and never had been except natural law, and that was not very much like book-law.

They had a fair view of the clearing. It seemed to be almost perfectly circular, about ten acres in size, but upon the far side a thin spit of trees barely screened an extenuation, over where still another meadow was.

The camp was northward where a little creek ran, smoke rose against a flawless, cold sky. The man was moving but not entirely discernible because of tall grass and the nearby background of trees.

Jess grounded his gun to lean on. Harris studied the camp, watched the movement, then said, 'I'll go first,' and stepped away from the trees heading diagonally toward the camp.

The man across the meadow had his back to Harris, bowed over his fire, but he swung almost immediately, warned by instinct. He was lean, wiry, and had neither been shorn nor shaved in a long time.

Harris raised a hand in casual salute. The stranger stood like stone watching and not responding. He had a saddlegun lying against a blanketroll, a shellbelt and holstered Colt. He also had a big belt knife. His hat was grimy, his trousers and shirt was worn and soiled, and by the time Harris got closer he could see the lines, the weathered look, and the small pale eyes above a hawkish nose and a wide slit of a mouth. He guessed the man to be in his forties. Late forties perhaps, but that did not have to be a good guess; people who lived outdoors invariably looked older than they were.

'Ridin' through,' Harris said from a distance, studying the stranger, his camp and his equipment. 'That fire looks good, friend.'

The stranger loosened a little, but cast a furtive glance in the direction of his bedroll where the saddlegun was lying. Then he said, 'Step up and get warm,' and ranged a probing look behind Harris. 'You alone?'

Harris smiled and shook his head. 'No. Are you?'

Instead of replying the stranger looked elsewhere, more intently this time. 'I don't see no one,' he muttered.

Harris unbuttoned his coat by the fire, raised an arm to gesture and his brother walked forth. The stranger stood watching Jess for a moment, then turned. 'Huntin' cattle?' he asked.

'No. Huntin' a bear.'

The stranger twisted to make his final appraisal of Jess, then leaned to poke some deadfall twigs into his fire. 'You won't find many out of their dens this time of year,' he said, and waited for Jess to come on up before

70

speaking again. 'I do a little huntin' and trappin' too. Mostly, this late, for hides with the hair well set.'

Harris introduced his brother and himself. The stranger nodded without smiling and finished stirring the fire before squatting by it to say, 'I'm Sam Garth. Do some rangeridin' in summertime, then head into the mountains in autumn for some early trappin', and hole up in whatever town I find for the winter.' He looked from Jess to Harris. 'I never been in these mountains before. You fellers familiar with 'em?'

'We've hunted them,' replied Harris, as Jess rummaged for his makings and sat down to build a smoke. Sam Garth watched Jess's every movement, and when Jess offered the sack and papers Sam Garth grabbed them.

'Been out of tobacco a long time,' he said, and built a smoke, held a firebrand for Jess, then lit up himself, inhaled deeply and exhaled. Then he smiled. 'By gawd, some things a man sure does miss.' He loosened a little more. 'I haven't seen no bear-sign since I been on this side of the mountains, except up high near the rims. In fact, by gawd, I been travellin' through here all day and haven't seen any kind of fresh sign. It's like all the game left out of here.'

Harris nodded. 'Do you know anything about grizzlies?'

Sam Garth's small eyes became fixed on

71

Harris. 'A little. Around here?'

'West of here but not very far. Somewhere west and south. Maybe between these uplands and the foothills. He's killed two men.'

Garth said, 'Jesus,' on an exhalation of bluish smoke. 'No game around. I figured maybe cougars or a wolf pack. You fellers seen him?'

'No. Just his sign and he's big.'

'Killed two men?'

Harris nodded. 'A cowboy southeast of here and an old man in the foothills. Darn near got a little girl too, and he's killed a saddlehorse and two cows.'

'You sure it's a grizzly? They ain't at all plentiful you know.'

Jess spoke drily. 'The little girl described him, and we've seen his kills.'

Sam Garth fingered his stubbly jaw while gazing into the fire. Harris and Jess studied him through the ensuing interval of silence before he spoke again. 'You boys ain't armed for grizzly hunting. Carbine won't do it unless you can set where he can't scent you and keep pumpin' lead into him. Then maybe it won't do it.'

Jess arose. 'I'll fetch the horses,' he announced and turned away. Sam Garth watched him briefly then faced Harris again.

'Mister, if there's a grizzly around and he smells horses...' Garth began to frown slightly, as though he might be regretting these visitors.

72

Harris's next question diverted him. 'You're on foot?'

This time Sam Garth seemed to briefly hang fire before responding. 'Yeah. I had a horse, but he died on me up near the rims. I cached the outfit, took my bedroll, carbine and grub and started walking.'

Harris nodded in sympathy, thinking that if this man was a trapper he'd eat his boots. 'How are you fixed for grub?' he asked.

Sam Garth jutted his jaw in the direction of the bedroll. 'Got two fat tree-squirrels in there I shot on the way down here.' He looked at Harris. 'But no salt. You boys got some salt?'

'Salt and some tinned peaches,' stated Harris, watching the other man's expression brighten. Then he said, 'If I was in your boots, Sam, on foot and all, I'd head north up away from this low-down country.'

Garth did not ask why, he merely nodded and reached for his bedroll to bring forth the squirrels.

CHAPTER EIGHT

THE TRAIL

Harris strolled out where Jess was having his after-supper smoke near the horses. Jess turned,

73

trickling smoke, and said, 'Hunter my butt. Did you ever see a hunter on foot wearin' rangerider's boots? I never did.'

Harris concurred. 'His horse died on him up near the northward peaks, he told me. He's a rangeman through and through.'

Jess said, 'Sure. Run to death—with a posse somewhere on the far slope lookin' for him, more'n likely. Well anyway, if he don't clear out of here before the bear smells him he's going to have to sprout wings.' Jess dropped the smoke and stamped it out, then raised a face showing disgust. 'He ate dang near that whole can of peaches.'

When they returned to the fire Sam Garth was hunkering there as though mesmerised. He glanced up and gestured. 'Fetch your blanketrolls in closer. It's goin' to be cold as hell tonight.'

They would have brought their bedrolls closer in any case but they did it now as Sam Garth begged tobacco from Harris and sat contentedly rolling a cigarette as his guests got their bedding over where heat would warm it. Then Harris went after more dry limbs in among the northward trees, and Jess leaned on his elbow staring into the fire as he said, 'They figure this bear's better'n a ton.'

Garth was not surprised. 'I've heard a lot of 'em got that big. But there can't be too many left. I've been ridin' out most of my life, in and

74

around the mountains, and I've never seen one.' He looked over where Jess had dumped the pack. 'Is that why you got that old buffler gun along?'

'Yeah. Forty-five-seventy.'

'You got bullets for it?'

'Nine.'

Garth faced the fire again. 'Maybe that'll stop him. It ought to at least slow him down. But I keep thinkin' you boys is most likely goin' to find a big black bear, not a grizzly.'

Jess yawned. 'Maybe.' He turned to unroll his blankets.

Harris returned with an armload of snag-wood, dumped it and fed several scraps to the fire. Sparks leapt, fire crackled, the radius of the heat expanded, and the three of them prepared to bed down.

The sky was clear, pale stars were glowing, forest-scent was on all sides, the horses were still gorging on the meadow close by, and somewhere at a great distance a lonely wolf sat back and sounded at the thickening moon. It was a long while before he was answered, and that second sounding came from off in the north-east somewhere, farther into the mountains.

Twice in the night Harris awakened and fed the fire. The trouble with sleeping in the mountains on a bitterly cold night was that only one side got fire-warmed and the other kept getting colder. But anything was better than a snowbank.

In the morning Harris pushed aside Garth's grimy little fry-pan and used Jess's, which was just as old and black, but was also cleaner.

They made coffee, something else Sam Garth had been without for some length of time. He seemed more cheerful at sunrise than he had seemed last night. He had gone out to look over their saddle stock and had been impressed. He told them horses like that would fetch almost fifty dollars over in Idaho, and when they were ready to strike camp and pack, he said he'd walk along with them for a while, that he'd been thinking about that bear and it seemed best for him to have company until he could get out of the area. He also asked if there were any cow outfits anywhere close by. They told him of Paul Jordan's ranch, which was southeasterly a number of miles, but the land boundary came up into the foothills directly below.

It bothered Harris to have someone walking on the same trail he was riding over, but it did not appear to bother Jess at all, and the reason may have been that Sam Garth had been smoking their tobacco and eating more of their grub than they had eaten since the previous night. It may also have been that Jess did not like the way Sam Garth admired their horses.

Harris aimed for the slope above the grizzly's territory. The mountainside was not as steep as

76

it looked from down on the flat plains of the cow range southward, and there were game trails by the dozen, some old, some new, some overhung with low branches, others with ample head-room for big bull elks in the rut. They used these elk trails.

When Jess called to his brother that they were high enough; that he had been watching for sign and had seen none, which meant the grizzly had to be a mile or two southward, Harris halted to study the lie of the land. His brother pointed in a vague manner.

'There's a park dead ahead and off the trail southward about a mile. It's got a salt lick. I've got my share of meat up there.'

Sam Garth was ahead in the trail. He started out again, carbine in one hand, taking springy steps. He was wiry enough to keep this up all day. They had his bedroll atop their pack on the mare.

Sunlight shone across the meadow, brilliant and cold. Some coyotes were out there worrying sinew off an ancient doe carcass. At sight of the trespassers they fled every way, startled out of their wits at the sight of three men in a place, where at that time of the year men almost never appeared.

Sam Garth halted suddenly in mid-stride, staring ahead. He slowly raised his saddlegun as a pointer. He was speechless. Easily seven feet from the spongy forest floor, upon the verge of the yonder park, was a ripped and clawed hardwood tree, its outer and inner bark shredded and mangled. He said, 'Jesus!'

Harris urged his mount closer, then shoved back his hat as Jess rode up. Laconically the younger Bolton said, 'That's a pretty tall black bear, Mister Garth.'

The wiry man had been looking elsewhere, on both sides as well as southward. When he faced the tree again, stepped up beneath those claw marks where a huge bear had been sharpening his claws while simultaneously looking for grubs, he said, 'Mister, if that was a black bear it'll be the biggest one anyone ever heard of.' He was looking up above his head at the slash marks. 'Didn't you fellers say he was down south in the foothills?', and before either of the Boltons could answer he also said, moving away from the bear-tree, 'This ain't no country for a man on foot.'

They had told him that last night. Now, they were studying the slash marks, their first sighting of anything to do with the grizzly, and ignored Garth.

Jess finally waggled his head. 'That's one hell of a big one,' he stated. 'How tall are you, Mister Garth?'

'Six foot even.'

'Those slashes were a foot over your head.'

Garth snapped his retort. 'I know that. I ain't blind. And they wasn't made too long ago.

78

Seems to me your damned bear's movin' up-country. Jesus!' Garth stepped over and put a finger into the closest slash mark. It went in half its length. 'And this here is a fir tree, not a pine. He's stronger'n a horse.'

'Two horses,' stated Harris, dropping his gaze to the spongy accumulation of needles underfoot, which muffled all sound and did not take impressions very distinctly, but this time the weight had been sufficient. He pointed. 'Turned off from here travelling on an angle along the slope, westerly.'

Garth snapped a comment. 'In that case, I'm goin' back the way we come. The opposite direction.'

Harris did not raise his eyes as he said, 'I wouldn't, Mister Garth. You go off alone on foot now...' Harris let it trail off as he urged his horse ahead past the tree. So far, none of the animals had showed anything more than a slight degree of uneasiness, and Harris was using this as his basis for a suspicion that the grizzly had ripped the fir tree the day before and had not tarried afterwards.

Jess rode around Sam Garth to follow his brother. Garth did not say another word, he simply trudged in Jess's wake.

The forest was shadowed but each clearing they reached was bright with cold sunshine, and the tracks were clearer out in the meadows. Garth stooped to measure one with fingers

79

extended the way men measured the size of a horse. When he straightened up his small eyes were round. He held one extended hand above the other and said, 'Jesus!'

Harris had the lead. He rode slowly and watchfully although as long as the ridgling did not check-up he was not too worried.

It was at a sump-spring where they found the most distinct set of tracks. This time Sam Garth stood looking without opening his mouth, but as they struck out again he began alternately studying Jess's mount and Harris's ridgling. He ignored the pack-mare.

An hour farther along Jess called a halt and said, 'Harris, that son of a bitch isn't holding steady, he's foragin' left and right.'

Garth interrupted. 'Bear that size, mister, has got to eat a hell of a lot each day.'

Jess spoke on. 'He damned well might cut back, and if he does he's goin' to pick up our scent.'

Harris said, 'Split up?'

Before Jess could answer Garth broke in to say, 'Don't do that. I'll tell you something—we'll make twice as much scent from different directions. He'll pick it up sure as hell. And pray don't no wind start to blow or he's goin' to smell us anyway.'

Harris and his brother exchanged a look, then Harris spoke. 'We got a choice, Jess. Find him before sundown, or get plumb out of his

80

territory, because after nightfall if he comes horse-hunting we're not going to be in too good a way.'

Jess gestured. 'Find him. Let's go.'

Harris nodded, turned and walked his horse out. The tracks from the seepage-spring went almost directly to a punky old deadfall, an enormous old tree which had simply died of age—and beetles. It was nearly six feet from the ground where it was lying to the topmost curve of its pceling bark. A man on foot could hide behind it without even bending his knees, if he was not very tall, and no horse in cow country could jump it. Here, the grizzly had spent some little time. He had torn all the way to the heart of the deadfall in his search for grubs. He had sweated and relieved himself and this time the horses were terrified, even the fighting horse under Harris. They had to leave the horses back a fair distance and go forth on foot to examine the deadfall, and as Garth climbed atop where the devastation was worst, he tossed down a lightweight piece of wood with dried blood on it. The bear had sustained an injury, not very serious evidently, during the course of his assault upon the old tree. Garth squatted up there, clutching his Winchester and looking in all directions. He said, 'You fellers are crazy. If he comes back and finds us, them horses of yours will leave the country, and leave you flat on your backs when they do it.'

Harris finished his examination of the tree and the fresher tracks, and led the way back to their horses. Here, he removed the old buffalo rifle from the pack, handing it to his brother. 'You got the bullets, Jess. You better load that thing.'

Now, the horses either still had the scent from the deadfall in their nostrils or had additional bear-smell in their faces as they renewed their way, because they walked lightly, prepared in an instant to whirl away and flee.

Harris unbuttoned his coat, tugged free the tie-down thong of his sixgun, shed his gloves and tugged his hat-brim down, hard.

It was a gamble whether they found the bear before he found them. It was also a gamble whether they could find him before sundown. The days had been getting shorter now, for more than a month.

Sam Garth suddenly said, 'No bear that big is the least bit scairt of men.'

Jess added something more to that. 'This one's not afraid of *anything*, and if he hurt his paw back on that deadfall, he's not going to be in a mood to do anything but charge.'

Garth's retort was curt. 'He'd charge anyway.'

Harris skirted a small meadow with a berry thicket in the middle of it. The thicket had been torn and trampled. On the far side Harris dropped down to pick up the sign again. From now on he had no intention of riding across any open country.

The tracks led across a muddied little trout-hole in some backwater beside a creek, then turned in a rough half circle. Jess spat, studied the tracks and shook his head. 'I'll tell you one thing Harris,' he said quietly. 'That son of a bitch's got our scent by now. Look there; he's cut back eastward below us.' Jess straightened in the saddle, held his horse in with a powerful hand, and made a sweeping gesture with an upraised arm indicating how the grizzly had gone down-slope, then had completed his half circle and was now travelling eastward. Then he dropped his arm. 'We got to do it before sundown, Harris. Now, we got no other choice. Otherwise he's goin' to come for us after the light fails. Sure as hell he's smelled horsemeat by now.'

Sam Garth stood slightly to one side tracing out the course of the downhill grizzly marks. He became quiet, which seemed out of character. When Harris turned down the hillside following the tracks Sam Garth did not follow. He cut diagonally across to intercept the horsemen farther along, where the tracks came back up-slope. Where the three of them came together Garth said, 'Listen, gents. You said there was a cow outfit south of here in the open country a few miles.'

'More like eight, ten miles by now,' stated

Jess.

Garth accepted this without question. 'All right. What we got to do now is head straight south down out of here, fast, head for that ranch, get us up a bunch of men and come back tomorrow. Maybe get us a dozen armed men.'

Harris had been studying the tracks. When the grizzly had made them he had not yet detected horse-scent or man-scent, and he had been moving on an uneven eastward course. Unless he cut back after picking up the scent, which was certainly possible, then he could still be travelling eastward toward the same area in the foothills where he had made his earlier kills—and that was between the hunters, now, and the Jordan ranch.

But Harris did not explain all this he simply said, 'He knows we're up here. If he's meat-huntin' by now I doubt that we could get out of the mountains, Sam.'

Garth's temper flared. It made his pale eyes icy and his stubby face malevolent. 'What you expect to do, just run aroun' like a gawddamned chicken with its head off, waitin' to get charged?'

Jess looked down. 'We didn't come up here to run from the bear, mister.'

Garth sneered. 'I'll tell you what, cowboy: that bear's goin' to string your guts out for fifty yards and scatter the rest of your carcass for another mile!'

84

Jess shifted slightly in the saddle eyeing the man on foot. When Harris was sure his brother was not going to reply, Harris said, 'This isn't helpin' at all. We got three carbines, a buffler rifle and three sixguns.' He waited while his brother and Sam Garth icily eyed one another a moment longer, then he lifted a reinhand. 'Let's go.'

Garth protested immediately. 'Not *that* way, for Chris' sake. Keep goin' west—away from him not toward him!' He flung out his arms. 'You fellers are ahorseback. Me, I'm afoot.'

Jess said, 'Then stay behind us, Mister Garth,' and turned his horse to follow Harris.

They had to slide and slip on the downgrade. Sunshine had cured the needles underfoot of last night's frost and the downslope footing was treacherous.

Harris turned to watch Sam Garth, whose leather-soled boots held no better than the calkless shoes on the horses. But they did not have to descend far, and as Harris picked up the fresh sign going easterly it was upon one of the innumerable game trails. From here on the footing was better.

But that was something else to think about; if the bear was indeed stalking them by now, and if they continued to remain on his trail, were in fact suddenly charged by him and the horses whirled to flee, in this kind of oily footing they would probably fall.

To correct this condition Harris tried to stay in among the darker parts of the forest where the footing was much better. But he could not always do it because they were following the bear, and *he* had not always done it. In fact, for a mile eastward he seemed to have been pursuing his own desires, which had to do with hunting for things to eat, and as often as he could he went out into the grassy parks. Then he stopped, churned the earth in one place for moments, and Harris nodded at his brother.. This was where the grizzly had picked up their scent. Jess nodded, sat still a moment to plug a load into the buffalo rifle and looked around where Sam Garth was watching.

CHAPTER NINE

A MISTING SKY

The sky had become misty with a miles-high overcast sometime during the early afternoon but no one noticed that. It was a little warmer too, and the air was as still as death.

There had been grey-squirrels among the trees but now there was not a sound of them, and that too went unnoticed as Harris kept the lead with Jess close behind balancing the buffalo rifle across his lap with his gloved right hand.

The grizzly's sign was fresher now and abundant. With nothing to fear, with the instincts of a pure destroyer, he had indiscriminately torn at trees, broken through thickets, left his sign almost as a challenge except that he was indifferent to that sort of thing. There was nothing in the mountains which would face him, even the gaunt big wolves who travelled in packs and could bring down almost any larger and more powerful animal. His hair was a matt of rank thickness teeth could not penetrate and his strength equalled that of ten wolf-packs.

They had increasing difficulty with the horses, particularly the pack-mare, so Garth took a lead-rope and pulled her along behind Jess until Harris finally halted, his seal-brown ridgling sweating as though he had been raced, with every nerve taut enough to make him quiver. They were getting close, there was no doubt of that. When they saw the grizzly nothing must divert them, least of all some frightened horses.

Wordlessly Jess dismounted holding the buffalo rifle. 'We got to leave 'em,' he said brusquely.

Sam Garth shook his head. 'If you tie 'em they're only goin' to bust loose and run down out of here. And if the bear's on his way back followin' a scent, he's goin' to find these horses and kill 'em, if they don't bust loose.'

It was true, but the Boltons had not come up here without expecting bad trouble and danger. Jess turned back leading his mount. Harris followed, so Sam Garth had to trail along too, with the pack-mare.

They found a tree-ringed thorny thicket and left the horses there, turned back on foot and now, finally, Sam Garth became silent. Even when they paused to talk, Garth did not offer a word.

Bear hunters in groups usually did not stay together. These three did; they had just one strength, their massed gunfire.

Where they stepped without sound through a tier of black firs something moved up-slope among a stand of saplings interspersed with aspen. The little trees quaked and Jess eased to one knee, waiting.

It was a cinnamon bear no larger than a big dog with blueberry stain across his muzzle. He suddenly reared up wrinkling his nose left and right, making little grunting whining sounds. He had their scent but could not see them.

They had to remain motionless waiting for curiosity to be replaced by fear. When that finally happened the little bear skittered up an aspen which bowed precariously under his weight. From up there, hunched over and clinging tightly, the little bear looked back and downward making steady sounds of fear and protest.

They passed beneath him in single-file.

Harris paused beside a huge tree to point southward and dead ahead. A tawny cougar was broken and bloody where something had shaken him out of a tree, had crushed him and stretched the body nearly half again its normal length. Blood was bright red and frothy.

Jess leaned to softly say, 'Why don't we hear him?'

Harris shook his head by way of answer, held his saddlegun in one hand while stripping the glove off the other hand, and finally said, 'Maybe he didn't scent us, Jess. Maybe he's not coming back but going on eastward.'

Jess looked doubtful as they began moving stealthily onward.

The high mistiness was steadily increasing, but so gradually it was unnoticeable, especially down beneath all those close ranks of stiff-topped huge trees. To Harris, whose eyes were accustomed to the hushed gloom, this visibility was better than bright sunlight would have been.

A fat badger backed up out of a dig he was making, turned with his nose-tip twitching, saw the Boltons, bared fangs at them then waddled back down where he had been working and began throwing out more dirt, backwards, as he burrowed. Pound for pound he was the fightingest animal in the mountains but he never attacked without provocation and the men were no threat.

He did not even back out for a closer inspection as the Boltons slipped past.

Distantly they caught the unmistakeable sound of wapiti or perhaps a band of deer. Preceding the panicked flight of these animals was the loud warning thump of a stag who had either seen or sensed peril, and had struck hard with a foreleg.

The unseen animals burst northward directly up the mountainside. They did not possess the lung-power to sustain this initial pace, but they could climb faster than any pursuing animal. Afterwards, all they had to do was maintain their lead.

Harris listened, marking their route and progress, then lifted his hat to mop sweat, re-set the hat and went ahead another few yards. It was beginning to worry him that, as Jess had mentioned, they had not as yet heard the grizzly. All bears were whiningly garrulous. Not this one. But he still should have been making audible sounds in the drawn-out silence through which the Boltons were moving.

Harris turned aside to say, 'We got to quarter for this trail. We got to have some notion where he is, or the son of a bitch is goin' to maybe come down on us from above or behind.'

Jess twisted to look back, and made a little breathless sound which brought his brother whirling on both boot-toes.

90

Sam Garth was gone!

For five seconds Jess remained motionless, then he turned fully to rake all their back trail which was in sight. When he still saw nothing he said, "The horses, Harris.'

They could go back, and arrive too late to prevent Garth's flight on one of their horses, probably driving the other horse ahead to prevent them from overtaking him, or they could continue the search, but whatever they did they were now on foot.

Jess let his breath out in a soft sigh. 'We don't have that much time,' he murmured. It was true; the day was moving along towards its end.

Harris's decision was reached more by instinct than by reason. They had perhaps two and a half hours of fair visibility left. The bear knew they were coming. If they turned back he would still know about where they were, at least he would be able to fix their general location by scent, and retreat would bring him along. Harris felt in his heart the grizzly was already stalking them. He had thought this for some time now, since it had become obvious that this giant killer who normally could not avoid making noise as he prowled, was now making no noise at all. This was undoubtedly the way he had caught those two cows. By getting close enough downwind to abruptly rear up and aim a disembowelling blow.

He was not a young bear, and the basic fact

that he was still alive was all the proof in the world that he knew all the feints and ruses of a successful killer.

Harris said, 'Let's get on with it,' and turned forward. Jess, who had needed nothing more to sway his decision about their course from here on, followed his brother on an angling descent toward an area of blowdowns, young, shallow-rooted tall trees lying like matchsticks in all directions where a freak storm had ripped through years earlier. There were small trees growing up through this maze of deadfalls, Christmas-tree-size. There were also thickets of thorny scrub brush. It was one of those forest areas all large animals avoided because of the difficulty in traversing it among the tumbled, criss-crossed dead trees and their up-ended medusa-headed butt structures with grainy roots thrusting lifelessly in all directions. But small animals throve here. They were generally safe, except from each other.

Harris was seeking sign when he came to the edge of this desolate place. When he looked up, for the first time he had a clear sighting of the sky. It held his attention for a moment. Jess had seen that sky. He said, 'Hell,' in a tone of deep disgust. 'I told you those In'ians were wrong. There's a storm coming.'

Harris turned to look elsewhere, then pointed to deep, fairly fresh smudges trailing off easterly at regular great intervals. The grizzly had skirted the area of the deadfalls. Harris turned to look back, then sank down upon a knee-high dead tree. 'Nothing as big as he is can keep quiet this long.'

Jess looked at his brother, beginning to frown. 'You don't believe that crap about a ghost-bear.'

Harris was scratching beneath his coat when he answered. 'No . . . But right now it wouldn't take a hell of a lot to convince me.' He swung sardonic eyes toward his brother.

Jess shifted the buffalo gun to the other hand and removed a glove, shoved it into a pocket and considered the old gun. It looked brighter now than it had in years, probably as a result of being rubbed and brushed against undergrowth on the way. He ran a hand along its thick barrel, wondering at its dull shininess. Then he straightened up in defiance of the odd mood which had just touched him, looked all around and settled beside Harris on the deadfall to say, 'I think we better stay right here. Him jockeying and us jockeying—it's goin' to end in his favour. We got to use the daylight that's left. He don't.'

'What you're saying is that we got to make him come to us.'

Jess agreed with that, then ran his hand down the rifle barrel again. 'It's not the hunt, Harris. I've done this a hundred times before. I got a strange feeling.'

Harris remained silent. He'd had that same

strange feeling for a while too, nor was it something he could pin down or define, but he settled for a partial analysis: death was very close, but not in a frightening way, rather in a manner that left Harris resigned, almost anticipatory; calm and fatalistically half-willing.

Jess broke across his brother's silence. 'You're right. He couldn't be this quiet.'

'If he's real he couldn't.'

Jess turned. 'That's gawddamned foolishness, Harris.'

Three striped chipmunks sprang upon their dead tree, halted in complete astonishment, and were absolutely motionless for perhaps five seconds, something very unusual in creatures as nervous as chipmunks, then they sprang back out of sight and made dead needles and corn-husk-dry leaves rattle as they fled.

From a distance there came another sound, this one made by a very large animal, west of where the Boltons were sitting.

Harris came up to his feet. His brother also arose, facing this new direction gripping the buffalo gun.

It was the sound of something crashing indiscriminately through a forest in furious pursuit. To Harris's knowledge there was no other animal but the grizzly who could make those sounds. 'West,' he said to Jess. 'He's west of us.'

His brother pointed using the buffalo gun.

'On our back-trail. Hell; I thought he'd be above us or maybe in front. He's went and picked up the scent back yonder. But he's goin' in the wrong direction.'

The answer to this puzzle came swiftly and suddenly. A muffled, flashing sound of gunfire burst the silence leaving no echo. Two shots; one, then after a moment the second one, then a terrible scream and a third gunshot, closer and followed by the terrified rush of an animal plunging eastward in scrambling terror.

'Toward us,' Jess said, and sank to his knee beside their deadfall as he raised the buffalo rifle.

There erupted a sound of animals breaking away in different directions, west and southward, but the predominant sound was of that scrambling run toward the area of the blow-downs.

Harris was sweating under his wool shirt. He got upon the far side of their deadfall, placed the saddlegun over punky wood with deliberate care, thumbed back his hat and bent low to snug oiled, curving wood to his shoulder. And wait.

The fleeing animal was holding to the trail. Behind him a larger beast was charging without regard for obstacles. Small trees snapped, underbrush was torn from the half-frozen earth, then the bear roared and Harris's knuckles around wood and steel whitened as his grip tightened to its limit.

The horse broke through into sight with a frothy red gash on its near shoulder. The rider was loose and doubled over, but holding mane-hair with both hands. The reins were torn close to the bit. Blood was flung up across Sam Garth's face from the horse's gushing wound, but even from a fair distance it was clear that Garth too was hurt. He flopped, held in place by a rider's lifelong instinct.

The horse could never have done it without having its pain-centres blocked. The shoulder was mangled. Each jump ahead showed wet, white bone moving through shredded meat.

Jess let the horse pass with a face drained of colour, tawny eyes down the riflebarrel fixed on the gloom farther back.

The horse slipped on needles, scrambled drunkenly and Garth lost his hold and fell loosely, like a grain sack. The horse struggled to regain its footing, then went past with blood streaming.

Harris was momentarily diverted where his brother had not been. Jess fired. The old rifle made a deafening roar. Its recoil half swung Jess and loosened his grip but in moments he recovered to lower the gun, tug open the breech, extract a greeny old brass casing and rummage in a coat pocket for a replacement. He did not once look up while he plugged in the second load and slammed down the breech, tugging back the hammer.

Harris had seen nothing to fire at, but when his brother shot Harris searched the forest for anything, size, movement, noise. There was nothing to aim at, just the back-trail with torn earth and blood on the tiny leaves here and there. Then silence.

Jess held the rifle low, cocked and ready. For moments he moved only his eyes. Then he spoke softly through stiff lips. 'I hit him. He got turned a little into a tree down yonder.'

Harris said, 'Where?'

Jess did not respond for a long while. Then he said, 'How in hell did he get Garth?'

This time Harris did not respond. He had no idea how the grizzly had done it, although he suspected that somehow or other the grizzly had got *around* Sam Garth and the horses, had gone up and around and had come down to the west where Garth would be fleeing. It was an eerie and frightening thought that a bear, *any* bear, could out-guess a man on horseback. But otherwise there was no way to understand why Garth had come charging *east*, with the grizzly behind him.

Silence returned, deeper than before.

They waited. Jess was watching the south slope where evidently he was sure the grizzly had gone.

Garth made a throaty, wet sound and feebly moved. For a while they ignored him, then Harris stood up, waited, and went forward to grab Garth's shoulders and drag him back upon the lower side of the deadfall.

Jess leaned over to look, and said, 'His back. Roll him over.'

The coat and shirt and soiled underwear beneath were in tatters. Garth's back from shoulders to belt-line was a jellyish mash.

'The horse was spinning away when the bear swung. He didn't catch the horse up high, he caught him a glancing strike on the shoulder. Maybe the second strike got Garth in the back. Harris, if that horse hadn't been moving that son of a bitch would have torn Garth in half.' Jess leaned to examine what was visible of the feebly moving man's back, then said, 'He's a goner,' as Harris dried bloody hands upon his trouserlegs.

The horse was gone. He might last another mile. Perhaps another two miles but no animal—or man—bleeding like that would last any more than two miles and most would not last half that long. It had been Jess's horse, which did not matter; Jess had already been afoot.

Sam Garth lapsed into deep unconsciousness, which was probably a blessing. Harris moved his arms and legs into normal positions and rocked back. They had nothing to make a bandage of and if they had had, the bleeding was beyond stopping.

CHAPTER TEN

GRIZZLY!

Jess Bolton was a man of little imagination and unalterable feelings. He had never liked Sam Garth from the time of their initial meeting at that campfire in the bitterly cold night.

He still did not like Sam Garth. The fact that Garth was going to die where he was lying on the cold needles beside a rotten tree did not alter Jess's sentiments about Garth. Nor did the fact of death in this form, or any form at all, change Jess's feelings. Finally, that Sam Garth had sneaked away, had stolen their horses knowing that he was putting them on foot against the grizzly, clinched it for Jess.

He watched his brother's earnest effort to stop the blood flow and dispassionately reiterated his earlier statement. 'He's a goner, Harris.'

Jess sat down on the tree moving his head and his eyes. The grizzly had evidently bypassed the scent of the Boltons in favour of a scent which meant food—the horses back yonder on the back-trail. It was probable that he had heeded Sam Garth's scent intermingled with the smell of horseflesh, and that made Garth's oncoming death ironic; he had been killed with indifference, not purposefully. He had simply been back there with the horses when the bear had gone for a kill to satisfy hunger.

If Jess had reasoned this way he probably would have made some dry remark to his brother. Instead, he sat on the tree looking and listening.

The bear was close, and now he would try to kill them also. When nothing happened, there was no noise and no movement, Jess began to speculate that the grizzly may have gone after the dying horse. His own blunt reasoning scotched that. Maybe, if he had not hit the bear when he had fired, the grizzly would have disdained them as he had with Sam Garth; would indeed have gone after the bleeding horse. But Jess hadn't missed. He had briefly seen the bear, had fired, had then seen the impact half twist the grizzly into a huge fir tree.

In pain, the grizzly would be out there somewhere in the dimming day licking his injury and becoming steadily more enraged.

Harris rose up on the opposite side of the log holding his carbine in stained hands. Jess shook his head indicating that he had heard nor seen nothing. He leaned for a look upon the ground at his brother's feet. 'Is he dead?'

Harris did not know. He did not believe so but he did not lean to make sure. 'Are you sure you hit him, Jess?'

'I'm sure.' Jess glanced at the old gun he was

holding. 'I'll tell you—I wasn't sure those old bullets would go off... It sounded like a cannon. It kicks like an army mule, too.'

Harris listened to a faint rattling sound at his feet, slowly glanced down, recognised the still flatness of a body which had no counterpart in life and said, 'He's dead.'

Jess twisted in the opposite direction to gaze southward. 'He knows we're up here, Harris. Maybe we'd ought to move deeper among the blow-downs. They won't stop him but they might delay him. Might slow him down.'

They left Sam Garth where he had died and went southward under the dun-tan sky with its strange opaqueness, down in among the awry trees and sprouting evergreens. Movement of any kind was a dead giveaway, but remaining in the relative open of this area's edge was worse. The grizzly could do as he had done with Garth, and with those dead cows, he could get around them and attack where they had little shelter or protection. They knew by now this three-thousand-pound animal had cultivated the knack of moving soundlessly.

If someone had told them a grizzly this size could pass through a forest without a sound, when he chose to, they would not have believed it. Now, they believed it, knowing that if they survived and told this to others, they would not be believed.

Some men did things in their lifetimes less

101

colourful people would never believe. It happened every day, somewhere.

The cold was increasing but visibility was better among the blow-downs. Occasional flourishing little replacement-trees growing up out of the humus provided by their predecessors hindered the view in some directions, but Harris did not stop until he was satisfied they had the best sighting possible, out here.

Jess leaned aside the buffalo gun long enough to rub palms briskly and say, 'It better end soon. It's going to snow.'

Harris squinted upwards, said nothing and wished he could make a smoke. Instead, he blocked in distant squares of territory examining each one for bear-shape or movement.

Jess said, 'Maybe I killed him,' but he did not sound convinced of this and Harris shrugged his disbelief too.

'If you didn't break a leg he's going to come, Jess.'

The young man muttered as he too turned to look. 'He better come soon. Daylight isn't going to last forever.'

A boulder rolling down-slope striking trees as it went erratically along indicated where some large animal may have dislodged it upon the lower side of the blow-downs. Jess hefted the buffalo gun and when silence returned with nothing more to hold his attention, he raised a hand to fasten the blanketcoat up around his throat.

'Do you remember the stories paw used to tell us about his hunts?'

Harris remembered. 'About that time he got treed by a black bear and his partner jammed his rifle.'

'Yeah. And the time he shot a buffler in a swale and walked down to bleed it out, and a war party of Arapahoes rode up onto the skyline drawn by his shooting?'

Harris smiled with his mouth, his eyes constantly watching. 'He should have written it all down.'

'Why?' said Jess, fixing his gaze upon a distant aspen thicket. 'You don't have any kids and neither do I. Who'd be around to read it? And after this is over maybe won't either of us be around to even get married, let alone have kids.'

'What's in those aspens, Jess?'

'You see anything? I been watching it.'

'There's something. . .'

Moments passed, the hush deepened, cold crept through everything the men were wearing to stiffen joints and muscles. Ice-cold steel in Jess's hand caused a dull pain so he shifted his hold of the buffalo gun.

Harris casually turned, twisting from the wait—and saw it—more than a ton of hair and muscle. In his calmest voice he said, 'Behind us,

Jess, up beyond the trail in among those big fir trees.'

But when Jess looked the grizzly was gone. There were dull layers of blackness up through there made darker now by failing daylight and the increasing overcast.

'I'll tell you one thing,' Harris said. 'You didn't break a leg. In fact he was moving on all fours like you didn't hit him at all.'

'I hit him, Harris. I saw the impact catch him in mid-stride and punch him off balance into a damned tree. You're sure it was him?'

'I'm sure.'

Jess shifted the rifle back to his right hand. 'I never even heard of a bear stalkin' men before. Did you?'

'No.'

'Where did he go?'

'East, over where all that darkness is.' Harris gently shook his head. 'He's damned awful big, Jess. Maybe these guns won't stop him.'

'They'll stop the son of a bitch, but a man's got to be able to get in a steady shot.'

Harris said, 'Not today, brother. When that grizzly's ready he's going to come at us like a freight train.'

Jess spat cotton. Cold or not he was thirty. He shot one swift glance upward, and when he lowered his head Harris was looking at him. He made a rueful face. 'Yeah, I know—why worry about gettin' caught up in here in a snowstorm.'

Without warning the grizzly roared. It was a sound to create a paralysis of terror in every animal within miles who heard it, with four legs or two legs.

Jess lifted the old buffalo gun and held it two-handedly across his body. 'The only sensible thing Garth said was about goin' back for a bunch of fellers with rifles.'

'Sure. But it was already too late when he said it.'

Harris raised a booted foot to the top of a dead tree and leaned, blocking in square of the northward territory. He had seen the bear, knew which direction it had been moving, thought he knew about where it had to be, but there was not a sign of it. Without turning his head he said, 'Yeah. That's what we should have done. Except that Paul Jordan wouldn't have stood still for a bunch of armed men crossing his range to come up here.'

Jess's reply to that was tart. 'The hell with Paul Jordan. We could have brought him along. He don't believe in grizzlies.' Jess smiled bitterly. 'No one believes in 'em around Canbyville. Right now I wish to hell some of those folks was standing here.'

Harris thought he detected movement, but it was much farther eastward than he had expected it to be. 'Jess? You see that woodpecker-snag to our right and down near the trail?'

'Yes.'

'Watch over there. Keep watching.'

Shadows were thickening throughout the uplands. Early dusk was coming and it would not last. This time of year dusk almost immediately blended with nightfall. Jess said, 'I don't see anything.'

Harris was undeterred. 'He's up there, making his way around to our right. Keep watching. He's got to cross the trail and when he does he'll be in the open.'

Jess knelt, moved here and there for a rifle-rest among the downed trees, and got into position to fire, head low, shoulders hunched, his body loose. Once he said, 'It's goin' to be tricky shootin', Harris, the light's gettin' bad.'

For Harris the wait was long and difficult. He leaned to try and skyline the trail, saddlegun held loosely ready.

The bear did not appear, nor could they hear him moving. He was out there, Harris was absolutely certain of that, but now he seemed to have changed direction. Harris turned very slowly. A terrified rabbit sprang into the air and lit down in a bound, sprang again and repeated his race, coming out of the northwest. He went within reach of Harris Bolton without seeing the man.

Harris felt hair on the back of his neck rising. The bear had *not* gone east, he had, somewhere up in the dark shadows, reversed his course. He was now west of them.

106

Jess lowered the buffalo gun to look around, then at his brother. 'Where?' he asked quietly.

Harris did not move when he replied. 'West, I think, Jess.'

'West?'

'Something scairt hell out of a rabbit. I think he's doubled back and is west of us now.'

'Harris,' exclaimed Jess in protest. 'Your attributin' to that bear human intelligence.'

'Watch west, Jess.'

The bear appeared, gradually, as though materialising out of murkiness as a part of it. He had heard the voices, was lifting and raising his head a little, testing for scent. He was down on all fours. Harris held his breath, unwilling to speak again and make it easier for the bear, but he wanted in the worst way to direct his brother's attention to the west. North of the crooked trail a little, and to the west.

The animal's head was massive; thick with a sloping skull from the little eyes upwards and backwards. The bear was thicker between the shoulders than any horse Harris had ever seen. He was two axe-handles across the back with a thick, huge body and his legs were oaken, slightly bowed in front, with feet showing great snags of claws.

Harris let his breath out slowly, took down a fresh big breath, and waited. Cindy Farnham had been right. That bear weighed more than a ton and was larger than any bear Harris Bolton had ever imagined.

The foetid odour came, finally. Harris remained motionless, momentarily too transfixed with the incredible sight up there across the trail to even raise his Winchester.

CHAPTER ELEVEN

DEATH!

One fact rooted itself in Harris's mind: no bullet by itself was going to bring that behemoth of a grizzly down. No gun a man could carry on horseback or raise to his shoulder would bring a bear that size down with one shot.

If they expended all their buffalo-gun ammunition, and hit the grizzly in his vital parts, they could do it, but their saddleguns were not going to even slow that bear down when he started his charge, unless...

Gradually falling shadows, increasing day's-end gloom, sifted down until the motionless bear was almost impossible to see. Then he turned with ponderous ease, each movement fluid and silent, sank from sight as he began a fresh manoeuvre, and Harris turned.

Jess was not still hunched near the rifle, he was half-erect with the rifle lying atop its log. When Harris moved Jess huskily spoke. 'There never was a bear that big.'

'You saw him too?'

'Yeah. He ain't alive, Harris, he's a nightmare.' Jess raised his eyes to his brother. 'Nobody's ever goin' to believe this.' Jess looked back up where the bear was, and kept looking up there. 'Remember what you said back down by my cabin? You sure as hell was right. We need a cannon.'

'How about a prayer?'

'They never worked for me, but go ahead if you want to.'

Instead, Harris looked farther back. They were almost in the middle of the blow-downs but in order to have the best visibility he had sacrificed the shielding cover of those little man-high third-growth trees. Now, he gestured, and as Jess nodded, moving farther back, Harris looked again for the bear.

He was not in sight, and clearly he was doing his stalking without the least concern for how long it might take him.

They had to clamber over deadfalls, and those which were too high for climbing had to be gone around at one end or the other. It was an impossible place to be in, if men had to retreat swiftly, but it was also a bad place for an enormous bear to charge through. He could not make speed and he could not charge directly at them.

Harris knelt, watching, thinking that they,

and the bear, had committed themselves to this place where neither could escape as long as the other remained alive.

Jess sighed and said, 'I don't know what the hell came over me. I could have shot.'

'You'll get your chance,' his brother retorted. 'What you got to concentrate on is not getting rattled when it's time to reload. That old gun is the best thing we got to slow him down.' Harris raised an arm to shove aside some bristly little pliable pine limbs and look out. 'You got to break a shoulder or a hip, Jess.'

The younger Bolton snorted softly. 'With that son of a bitch coming straight at a man he's got only two choices—head-shot or heart-shot.'

Harris did not pursue this. His brother knew as well as he did that a head-shot on a big bear was unlikely to bring the animal down, especially from in front if the bear had his head lowered in a charge.

Visibility was fading slowly. That overcast sky seemed more sooty now but the temperature had not dropped in the last hour. The air was utterly still and the silence which had been deepening, was now almost physical; the grizzly's smell had completely surrounded the area of the blow-downs, and had permeated elsewhere in all directions. Animals such as elk and deer which relied upon flight, had fled long ago. The smaller creatures were either deep underground or deep in their tree-holes. The grizzly had come to dominate this entire area.

Harris eased back, let the pine limbs resume their normal position, looked behind, southward, then responded to the gentle nudge of his brother and followed Jess's stare to the east.

'It's him,' the younger man said in a low half-whisper. 'I think I know what he's doing. Going around us, first one way then the other way. He's jockeyin' back and forth to confuse us ... I don't believe this bear, Harris.'

The elder Bolton thought of reminding his brother of Jess's earlier scoffing when he had accused Harris of attributing human intelligence to the grizzly. Instead, he sank to one knee, grounded his Winchester and waited, occasionally looking elsewhere.

Jess was wagging his head a little. 'I *know* I hit him, but he sure don't act like I did.'

From a great distance a sound rode eastward on the frigid air, little more than a series of diminishing shockwaves. It seemed to come from the southeast, down somewhere in the vicinity of the foothills. Jess said, 'What was that?' and his brother shook his head by way of an answer. He had no idea what it was, and at this particular moment he did not care.

The bear roared. It was like a blast of sound coming from a large instrument under great pressure. Trees shattered the echo but the Boltons pinpointed the sound's direction. It was

111

indeed east of them.

This time, however, Harris eased around more southerly. Before, each time the bear worked in closer during his surrounding tactic, he had moved immediately after roaring. Downhill was easiest now, for the bear, and it was also the most reasonable route because from the lower end of the area he had the best access; the deadfalls down there, jumbled, criss-crossed and indiscriminately jumbled atop and across one another, were much smaller than they were elsewhere.

Jess was still waiting, his eyes fixed to the east. Harris could hear his brother's breathing.

But nothing happened southward. Time passed, Harris shivered from inactivity in the cold, wavered in his conviction of the bear's latest move, and glanced over at his brother. Jess was also shivering. When their glances met Jess said, 'If he don't come soon, Harris, it's goin' to get too dark to see him even when he charges.'

The bear broke clear of the northward trees. He had not gone southward down around the area of the two forted-up men, he had turned back northward, had half-circled the territory and being satisfied his ruse had worked, had decided to attack.

They had an early warning because in his charge the giant meat-eater could not avoid making noise. They swung, surprised at the position of the grizzly, and saw him break clear of the forest heading toward them at a shambling run which was picking up momentum as he came down into the trail and across it.

He swung massively from side to side. His head, nearly flat between the small black eyes, and sloping back, which was the same size as his columnar neck, was lowered. Except that he was gaining speed as he crossed the game-trail and was therefore discernible in the black gloom behind him, they would have been unable to make out the hugeness of his body.

He had his winter coat, which made him appear even larger, but there was little time to notice details. He came to the first blow-downs, which were middling-sized trees, and with fluid suppleness, and a deep-down grunt, sailed over them, hit down upon the far side and with little more than a momentary check to his impetus, swung an enormous paw and shattered the next punky dead tree with a shower of pithy splinters and dun dust.

Harris snugged back the carbine, hunched his body around it and fired for the body. He was levering up when to his right Jess's buffalo gun nearly deafened him. The bear plunged ahead where he had broken that punky deadfall, and without flinching, as far as either man could see, came down over the next pair of criss-crossing dead trees.

Harris settled to fire again, taking longer to aim this time, trying for a heart-shot with his Winchester. The bear nearly dropped from sight just as Harris fired. He had come down upon the far side of those piled-up, jumbled trees into an erosion gully upon the far side. The ditch was deep enough to hide any ordinary big black bear. The grizzly's entire curved massive back was in sight when Harris fired. If he scored at all it had to be a searing, raking scratch down the length of the bear's back.

The bear reared up on his hind legs to lunge out of the gully. He was close enough now so the men could see details of his body. His nose was deeply scarred and his forehead had a sunken place directly above the eyes. It could have been the result of a dented skull from a horse-kick.

He came up over the next series of deadfalls directly ahead. He could not see the men but he had seen muzzleblasts. With an enraged roar he struck left and right at hindering blow-downs which were all rotten and punky, and broke to bits under his blows but still hindered his charge.

Jess fired again, his second round since the bear had come across the trail, and this time he missed. He and his brother both saw the explosion of gall-wood where the huge lead slug hit a yard to the grizzly's left side.

Harris levered up, fired and levered up to fire again. He knew he was scoring but it was like a

114

series of bee-stings; the gigantic mankiller kept coming. There had to be bleeding but it was not visible in the matt of thick winter fur, and the poor light.

There was still a hundred yards separating the men from the bear when Jess, slamming down the breech of the buffalo gun, called to his brother. 'We're not goin' to do it! We're not goin' to down him!'

Harris, keeping track of his carbine-shots knew he was getting close to the end. He had more saddlegun slugs in his shellbelt, in back, but they might as well have been back down on his desk at the Canbyville jailhouse; he would not have time to reload.

Jess took long aim and fired. Harris's ears were still ringing from the earlier gunblast on his right. This time, as the grizzly was rearing up to lunge across more jumbled dead trees, he seemed to momentarily falter. But it could have been an illusion because the very next moment he came down across the trees.

They could smell him despite the blackpowder smoke hanging in the air around their position. Harris had nothing but an immense shaggy, foul-smelling body directly in front when he fired his final round from the carbine, then sprang up to swing the gun in an arc and hurl it. The bear's upper foreleg met the gun in mid-air. The gun bounced as though it had struck stone. Harris drew his sixgun as the bear came crashing down across a litter of piled trees, with only one more such jumble to cross before he reached the spot where the men were.

Jess jumped up holding the buffalo rifle with both hands at the hip. His face was grey to the hairline. He did not yield a single step even when Harris yelled at him to run southward, and started to set an example by one-handedly hurdling the downed trees behind them. Then Jess fired as the grizzly came up onto his hind legs, towering above the final jumble of downed trees.

The bear roared. He was close enough now to show red froth in the slobbers of his open mouth.

Jess turned, sprang over the rearward tree and followed Harris in a flinging rush to get yardage between himself and the bear so that he would have time to reload.

The grizzly finally saw them. His eyesight was not good at best; he hunted by an extraordinarily acute sense of smell, and when he was close enough to prey to see it, he was also almost close enough to make one of those mighty sweeps with his forelegs.

Harris fell, rolled frantically in the forest-litter and came up with a bleeding left hand which he used to lever himself upright with as he turned back to aim with his handgun. This time, the muzzleblast was louder and the flame was blindingly intense. The bullet of a single-action .45 was one of the slowest moving there was; its lethal ability came from the way, after it began to lose momentum, out a short distance, it began to tumble end over end. It made a terrible wound when it hit flesh tumbling like that.

But the blinding muzzleblast was what appeared to momentarily divert the huge meat-eater. His weakness was his eyes. He teetered, great forelegs up, his entire thick torso towering into the settling dusk, red froth on his muzzle, then he roared and dropped forward across the last tree-barrier.

Jess was reloading with icy calmness. He did not even raise his eyes when the bear roared, but his body quivered. Then he slammed down the breech and hauled back on the hammer.

The bear was past and through that final tree-wreckage when Harris, slightly to one side of his brother and behind him, saw Jess raise the rifle and sight down its barrel. He fired; the impact jerked Jess backwards, his bootheel struck a half-buried pine-knot and he fell backwards, trying to twist sideways as his body turned in falling.

The bear came up to his full height. Harris had to raise his head to look into the slobbering mouth with its rows of bone-white teeth. He had no idea whether Jess's last shot had taken effect but as the bear reared up he roared with his head swinging from side to side.

Harris dived for his brother, caught loose cloth of the blanketcoat and set back to pull with all his strength. Jess slid free and made a lunge for the buffalo rifle as he was wrenched away. Then he too looked up. The bear was beginning to drop forward, forelegs wide and inward-curving. He had both black eyes fixed upon the younger Bolton.

Harris let go of the sixgun to use both arms in pulling his brother desperately away as the bear came down onto all four feet. Harris's lungs burned from straining. Jess broke away and rolled over and over to the east, to his left, still clutching the useless, fired-out buffalo gun. The bear swung his body to the left, heaved his immense weight onto his left leg and raised the right one to strike.

Harris saw the blow reach his brother. Jess was lifted bodily and flung like a broken doll. The buffalo gun fell away as Jess's body struck atop a downed tree, sagged there, then slid inertly down behind the deadfall.

Harris moved, kicked his sixgun, scooped it up as the bear turned toward him, his attention diverted by movement.

The bear did not rear up this time. He took two huge forward steps, crushing the body of a downed tree with weight alone, and with blood running from his nose and mouth, altered stance to strike with his other foreleg. Harris, without time to glance back, sprang backward. He did

118

not fall and the bear's lunging strike missed by inches, but Harris's hips were dead against a waist-high log at his back.

The bear recovered and moved into position for another sweep. Harris cocked the sixgun and fired at point-blank. The brilliance nearly blinded him. The bear froze, ready to swing his foreleg.

Harris saw the black eyes open and close several times rapidly. The bear had been blinded. He had also been hit but he showed nothing now either, when a bullet had ripped into him.

Harris acted upon a desperate gamble, the only chance he had now. He sidled along the treetrunk to his left, kept moving and watching to see if the bear could determine what the man was doing. The grizzly was blinking and snuffling and weaving his gigantic carcass left and right as though uncertain.

Harris had three slugs left. He sidled clear, then started forward toward the right side of the grizzly. He had the sixgun raised and cocked. The bear heard him coming, lumbered heavily as though to shift stance, and Harris fired directly into his face. The bear's head dropped instinctively from the muzzleblast's eye-searing light. Harris cocked the gun and took two closer big steps, shoved the gunbarrel under the ear of the bear and fired again, cocked the sixgun for his final attempt, and moving the barrel six or seven inches fired directly into one of the little black eyes.

The bear hung there, still rocking from side to side, then lunged ahead, falling across the juncture of where three rotten trees criss-crossed each other. His weight crushed all three of those punky treetrunks.

Harris was shaking like a leaf, empty, cocked sixgun dangling from numb fingers. He had to reload. He told himself that, over and over, before his nerves and muscles would respond. He had to reload, then he had to find Jess.

He could hear bubbling, wet gusts of breath coming from the bear lying three feet in front of him as he used cold-stiff fingers to shuck out six spent handgun casings and plug in six fresh loads from his shellbelt.

Finished with the reloading, slippery with icy sweat beneath his clothing, he moved a little and watched the bear for reaction to the sounds he had made. There were none; the huge animal was beginning to occasionally quiver his full length.

Harris stepped around in front to face the bear whose one good eye was dulling over. There was still an infrequent burst of bubbly froth from the nostrils.

He extended the sixgun for a final shot, stood a moment like that, then eased off the hammer, stepped back and let go a shuddering breath before turning on leaden legs to find Jess.

CHAPTER TWELVE

ON INTO THE NIGHT

The icy air smelled of punky dust, gunpowder and boar-bear, and if terror had had a smell, it would also have smelled of that, as Harris stumbled his way over behind the deadfall pine where he had seen his brother slide out of sight.

The only discernible sound for a long while was made by Harris's bootsoles crunching over freezing twigs and crumbling earth.

Jess was lying in a pile, his body half against the tree, his face and shoulders to one side as though he were sleeping.

Harris knelt, pulled his brother away from the tree and stretched him out into a normal position. Starlight would have helped but there was none and as Harris leaned to begin a close examination, something white drifted down to fall upon the back of one hand.

Jess's breathing was shallow and fluttery. His unconsciousness was deep. Harris unbuttoned the blanket-coat, the woollen shirt beneath, looking for torn flesh and blood. He found none on the torso and looked elsewhere, then he re-closed his brother's clothing and sank weakly down, with both shoulders against the dead tree, with an almost overpowering desire to

121

sleep.

Whatever Jess's injuries, they were not external. Harris gazed at his brother, turned gradually to look at the dead bear, and finally lifted his face into the lazily falling, occasional snowflakes. He was wrung out through and through, more exhausted than he had ever been before in his lifetime.

It required physical effort just to fish around under his jumper for the tobacco sack in his shirt pocket, and to afterwards roll and light a smoke. From time to time his body shuddered from head to toe, but he controlled that after a while. He also forced himself to stand up and look around.

The route of the grizzly's charge was clearly discernible even in the sickly gloom of an oncoming storm, all the way from the northward trail down through the area of the downed, dead and jumbled pine trees.

He killed the cigarette and went over to consider lifting his brother. But Jess was a large, heavy man. Another time Harris could have done it. Not now. Still, they had to get up out of this tangle of dead timber before the snow filtered in to cover all the pitfalls. He breathed deeply, turned his back to the huge dead animal on his right, studied the grainy sky and concentrated on physical recovery. It took a long time. Once, he heard a distant noise to the east, and ignored it. On nights such as this one was, freezing treelimbs would burst with the sound of a gunshot. Maybe that was what it had been. He turned, looked at his motionless brother, and leaned to grab hold. The hardest part was lifting. Once he had Jess up across a shoulder he could stagger ahead, but it took time; they had retreated deeper into the deadfall-area than he remembered. He rested twice by leaning his burden upon a downed tree, then started forward again.

When he reached the trail his lungs were close to bursting, his heart was dangerously hammering in its dark place, and he had to reach for an upright fir tree with both hands to remain standing.

Jess groaned. His stubbled features grimaced in pain.

Harris knelt and pulled the blanketcoat closer around his brother's throat, but the cold had not been increasing for a couple of hours now. It was still well below freezing, and to an injured man suffering pain and shock, it could be enough to bring on complications so Harris shed his jumper to make additional shelter for Jess.

His feet hurt from cold inside their boots and his fingers worked stiffly when he lifted Jess's head and shoved a mound of needles beneath for a pillow.

Jess ground his teeth with an audible sound. When Harris leaned down Jess opened his eyes looking directly upwards. There was no interval of drifting back to awareness. No moment for wandering eyes to focus. He looked straight upwards and said, 'Where is he?' in a tone of crumbling effort. 'Harris . . . ?'

'He's dead, Jess. We killed the son of a bitch. He's back down yonder among those deadfalls . . . Where do you hurt?'

Jess was momentarily silent, his eyes drifted to the treetops and drifted back slowly. 'Hurts like hell to breathe,' he said.

Harris nodded. As he now recalled it, the bear had caught Jess on the rise, to the side of Jess's body as his brother had been wrenching half around in flight. 'Maybe it's busted ribs,' he told Jess. 'I hope to hell that's all it is. I'm goin' to hold your head up. Spit in my glove.'

Movement was painful but Jess obeyed. There was no blood in the palm of the soiled glove. Harris eased Jess's head back down and his brother unclenched his teeth to say, 'It's snowing . . . Harris . . . ?'

'Don't worry about it, Jess.'

'We got no horses. It'll have us snowed in come morning.'

Harris forced a smile. 'We got enough dead wood around here to keep warm until next spring if we got to. Quit worrying.'

They looked at one another for a moment, then Jess let his eyes tiredly close. 'The buffler gun,' he muttered, and did not explain what that meant.

124

Harris stood up, stamped his aching feet and looked around for kindling. Whatever else happened, they had to have a fire. He thought only of that until he had accumulated enough dry wood to light it. Then he concentrated upon bringing in more and more armloads of wood from among the deadfalls behind them.

Finally, he stood in the wonderful warmth and flickering light with time to think of their real peril. If the snowfall increased and kept up all night, was a foot thick or more by morning, for him to carry his brother down out of here was going to be impossible.

He could build a travois, load Jess onto it and try pulling over the snow on the game-trail. It was a chance; a weak one which depended upon how deep the snow would be by morning, and also upon his personal strength, but if there was any other way for them to get down out of the mountains his tired mind did not find it.

Jess awakened, squinted at the blaze and seemed to be feeling better. Harris rolled a smoke, lit it, wondered idly what time it was, and went over to squat by his brother. 'Are you hungry?' he asked, and Jess answered in a normal voice, which was encouraging.

'Naw. But I could eat, I guess.'

'How do you feel?'

'Better. My side hurts; I guess you're right, he did bust some ribs, but as long as I'm warm and don't move, don't breathe too far

125

down . . . . Harris, what happened down there?'

'I wasn't watching too close, Jess, but I think you hooked a foot into a snag and fell. Something like that. Anyway, when you floundered around he swung. I saw him boost you into the air and I saw you come down on your side and back and head, then roll off the log.'

'And then?'

'I shot the son of a bitch.'

'With the buffler gun?'

'No. With my sixgun. I blinded him with muzzleflash. When he was blinkin' and tryin' to see me, I got off on his right side and shot him in the ear, then in the eye. . . . Harris took back his coat close and stared at the fire. 'It didn't kill him, Jess.'

'Two bullets in the brain?'

'Yeah, two in his brain. But it destroyed his ability to move, to make his legs move. He fell forward finally. He was still blowin' air and blood ten minutes later. Then I guess he died.'

Jess also stared into the fire. 'You know, Harris, right now when it all happened just a little while ago, I'm already beginnin' to doubt the size of that bear . . . The light was bad and he kept movin' and I know damned well there never was a bear that big.'

Harris smoked, let heat work its wonderful way through his garments and into his body, which had not been warm since they had first ridden out, and made a little laugh. 'I'll tell you somethin' Jess. We're not goin' to be able to prove it.'

'Yeah; they won't find any of us under ten feet of snow until maybe next summer.'

Harris shot back an angry retort. 'No! What the hell are you talkin' about! We'll make it down out of here. Hell, it's only about fifteen, eighteen miles to the open country ... What I meant was—varmints up in here are goin't to live off that grizzly carcass all winter, hair, hide, guts and all. By summer there's not goin' to be anything left but a few bones wolves'll scatter for ten miles.'

From somewhere to the east a faint sound rode across the crackling of their fire, indistinct and muffled. Harris looked in that direction across the twisting, darting tendrils of orange flame, and leaned to pitch in more wood as he said, 'Dead tree toppling,' and raised his head to look at the trees around their spectre of red-orange heat, in the dark stillness where snowfall limited their vision.

Jess was still thinking back. Whatever had made that sound did not distract him. 'Paw's buffler gun,' he said.

Harris sat comfortably for a while, then groaned and got to his feet. 'I'd better get it while it's still above the snow,' he said, and turned away from the fire, whose light reached well down into the area of dead trees where they had killed the grizzly. He also went after his own gun, and Jess's hat if he could find it.

The bear had moved. He had crushed through the deadfalls upon which he had landed when his legs had turned loose, but now he was several feet farther along, and was lying half on his side as though sleeping.

It made hair stand up on Harris's neck. Nor did he make his gun-hunt without always being in a position to see the carcass from the corner of his eyes.

He found the buffalo rifle, his own carbine and his brother's hat. He stood off a short distance gazing at the bear. There was congealing blood, turning black against the snow around the grizzly's head. No amount of temptation could have got Harris to go over and touch the bear, even with an extended gunbarrel.

He looked at the grainy sky, thought he made out several obscure stars up there through a series of misty, shroud-like clouds which were breaking up and reforming as they moved southward, then, with the cold beginning to work into his joints and muscles, he turned back in the direction of the fire.

Jess watched his approach. The fire was bright and burning brighter as pitch-pine noisily took off sending forth gouts of oily black smoke.

Harris put the guns down and dropped his

brother's soggy, crumpled hat where it would dry, sat down and said, 'You can get a better idea of his size where he's lyin' surrounded by snow.'

'Is it coverin' him?'

'No.'

Jess did not take his eyes off his brother. 'What do you mean—no? If he's dead he's getting cold and the snow'll stick, Harris.'

'Well, so far it hasn't begun to stick.'

'Then by gawd he isn't dead!'

Harris leaned and shoved cold palms to the fire. 'I don't want to talk about that son of a bitch for a while, Jess ... We got to figure ahead. The fire's fine and all, but we can't get by with just heat. We got enough strength, I guess, to make a run at gettin' down out of here after dawn.' Harris pulled his hands back and rubbed the hot glove-leathered palms together turning slowly to face his brother. 'I'll make a travois as soon as I can see good enough to find some saplings.'

Jess lay back in long silence. After a while he said, 'I can walk. Busted ribs don't keep a man from doing that.'

'Not very far in a foot of snow, Jess.'

'We'll see, come daylight ... I sure don't like the notion of that son of a bitch still bein' alive, Harris.'

'He's not alive.'

Jess turned his head, seemed about to speak,

then simply lay their gazing at his brother. Harris felt the look and loosened his coat to the warmth. 'He's dead. Maybe it just takes longer for the body heat to go out of bears that size.' The pitch-pine was guttering low now, dropping flaming little bits of hissing pitch into the ash. 'Jess; now I know why those old time In'ians made such a big story out of killing grizzlies. It goes beyond just bear-killing.'

Out in the eastward night a man's voice came thinly in a fluting call cutting across the snow-hush. Firelight on a night like this was visible a long distance, but the smoke-scent was discernible even farther.

CHAPTER THIRTEEN

NEARING THE END

There were three of them leading two saddlehorses, with Paul Jordan out front by a couple of yards, and each rangeman had a shawl tied across the crown of his hat, down each side and knotted beneath his chin where coat-collars were turned up.

Their horses breathed steam as they arrived in the firelight-visibility on the game-trail which went eastward.

Jordan sat a moment gazing at Jess, then at

Harris, and finally he came stiffly down from the saddle and stepped closer as he said, 'We got your ridgling, Harris, and we found your pack-horse with stuff scattered for a mile back toward the foothills.' He pulled off his gloves, slowly. 'On the way up here, Jess, we found your horse—dead down the trail a mile or so. I don't see how he got that far.' Jordan turned as his riders eased up, one leading the seal-brown moving up and around while seeking a place to tie the ridgling.

'Sounded like a damned war,' a wizened, slightly stooped older rider said, his thin body bulky with clothing. He grinned, little shrewd eyes wandering down to Jess. 'You hurt?'

Jess knew the older man. 'Howard, by any chance you got some whisky?'

The older man kept grinning and jerked a gloved thumb in Jordan's direction, then walked off to tie the ridgling, and suddenly whipped straight up making a loud ejaculation *'Gawd'a'mighty!* ... Paul, there's a dead feller over here!'

Jordan turned, then walked over and looked in silence. The third rangeman also had to see Sam Garth. Jordan walked back and extended his hands to the fire. 'Who was he?'

'Feller named Sam Garth,' Harris said, and briefly explained about Garth; how they had met him, what he had been like, and finally, how Garth had run back to take a horse and free the other horses in his bid to get out of the mountains.

'And the bear got him,' stated Jess quietly. 'Along with my horse.'

Jordan went to his saddlebags, rummaged, then returned with a bottle of whisky when he leaned to hand first to Jess. As he straightened up looking at Harris he said, 'Well; we figured there'd be just the two of you. The snow's stickin' back yonder so we can't kill too much time up here, and it's goin' to overburden someone's horse haulin' double.'

Jess handed back the bottle. 'Leave him,' he growled, still hostile toward Garth even though the man was now dead and stiff, with snow sifting over him.

Jordan did not pursue the subject. He turned to look southward. 'We could hear you fellers shootin' five miles. Where is it?'

Harris, anxious to get down from here, pointed. 'Down there among the deadfalls. Go look, Paul.'

Jordan walked away, then turned back to hand the bottle to Harris before starting out again. Both his rangemen went along, their crunching footfalls solid in the quiet night as Harris tilted his head, swallowed, then lowered the bottle to find Jess gazing up at him. He smiled and Jess winked, then they waited.

Jordan returned. His riders stood in flickering red firelight with congealed expressions and Paul Jordan opened his coat to the heat as he said, 'I never in my life saw anything like that. I never saw an animal that *big*. Not even among my bulls. Lord'a'mighty, it *was* a grizzly.' He kept staring into the fire. 'Did he get you, Jess?'

'A little. Busted some ribs, I think.'

'And that dead feller—and your horse . . . ?'

Harris mentioned the rider named Crippen, then took down one final pull on the bottle and handed it back to his brother, who also took one more swallow.

The wiry man squinted around. 'We better start back, Paul.'

Jordan nodded, taking back his bottle to pass it to his riders, then they got the horses ready. Jess did not make a sound as they lifted him to his feet, allowed him a moment of standing, then with rough gentleness boosted him astride. He had his shapeless, filthy old hat shoved forward and pulled down almost to his ears, the blanketcoat snugged to the gullet and his gloves on.

Jordan looked back at them all before mounting in the lead. Harris had the bent, stiff body of Sam Garth behind his cantle lashed there with lariats. The rangemen had the guns Harris had retrieved. Paul hauled himself up, sat, then eased ahead in a walk.

Harris watched his brother but Jess was bundled and sitting up there without making a

133

sound, his face hidden by hatbrim-shadows.

Snowflakes, smaller than they had been originally, drifted slowly in all directions cutting off the view even dead ahead, but the slopes on both sides, to the north and the south, were bisected by a flatter place where the game-trail wound among trees whose topmost branches were beginning to bow under wet-weight.

Harris looked for those stars he thought he had been able to make out earlier. There was nothing up there now but snowfall; he could not see any sky at all.

His ridgling had not made a fuss when Garth had been lifted into place and tied fast. Probably, under better conditions he would have, but it was close to morning, bone-chilling-cold, and he had been both frightened and hungry for a long time now. There was not much testiness left. He plodded along behind the horse of that wiry old rangerider, head down and legs moving with stolid cadence through snow which was ankle-deep.

Except for the whisper of leather rubbing over leather, and shod hooves crunching through snow build-up, there was not a sound for a long while. Jess asked for the bottle as they passed across a park, and Paul passed it back without reining up.

Harris refused the offer when his brother had finished so Paul took the bottle back. Then he said, 'This snow'll keep 'em out, Harris. The

134

men from town who'll want to see that bear.'

Harris did not respond. The whisky had warmed him less than it had relaxed him. Now, he was fighting off drowsiness.

'Harris?'

'Yeah, Paul.'

'I—uh—got a bad habit of shootin' off my mouth sometimes.'

'I guess we all have.'

'I mean about what I said in the yard out front of the barn.'

'I knew what you meant. Forget it.'

'All right.' Jordan cleared his throat, then drank and shoved the bottle down into his saddlebag without noticing the look of reproach in the eyes of his two riders. 'We can make it down to the ranch,' he told them all. 'The horses were shod with calks couple weeks ago, so we can go down-slope without much fear of falling.' He twisted to glance at Jess without saying anything more.

They had to stop when Jess began to wilt in the saddle. The snow was falling with greater intensity now, soggy and clinging. The trail was frozen beneath but mushy on top, which slowed progress, but as Jordan had said, with calked shoes there was less danger of falling. It *could* happen, but it would not happen as readily.

Jess's condition was deteriorating. They removed him from the saddle and broke pine boughs to place him upon, on his back, and Paul took Harris aside to say, 'I don't know . . . We're less'n half way. Maybe it's more'n busted ribs.'

That fear had been eating at Harris since his rough examination after he had first found Jess unconscious behind the punky tree.

Jordan looked southward. It was barely possible to see open country below and southward, a great white blanket of it. They had tipped down off the mountainside at a steady walk and were close enough to the open range to be encouraged. But Jordan's home place was still a considerable distance off. And besides that, visibility was distorted in this kind of weather, even with snowfall to impair it. They were nowhere near as close to the ranch as it seemed they might be.

'I'll stay here with him,' Harris said of his brother. 'When he's able we'll start out again.'

Jordan shook his head over the suggestion. 'He might not be able to straddle a horse for three, four hours, Harris.' Jordan turned to the youngest of his rangemen. 'Galt, go on ahead. Make time. Hitch up the feedin' team to a wagon and head back. We'll maybe be able to meet you in the foothills. We'll head for red rock.'

Galt turned to mount up. They watched him, except Jess, who seemed to no longer care about anything. As Galt reined around them on the trail Jordan said, 'Pitch in some straw.' Galt nodded and rode onward.

Jordan crunched back to stand looking down at Jess Bolton. Whisky would no longer help. Nothing would, except Jess's own inherent strength, and that had been depleted since sundown the previous night. The wiry cowboy stepped up to say, 'If we're goin' to stay I'll hunt up some firewood.' Jordan shook his head. 'We're goin' down at least to the foothills, by hook or by crook.' But that was all he said, except to mutter something about wishing his rangeboss were here.

Harris squatted beside his brother. Jess was comfortable, apparently, but the cold would come up into him from the frozen ground he was lying on, pine-boughs notwithstandng. Jordan was right; they could not remain up here much longer. He leaned and spoke.

'Jess? Can you hear me?'

The reply came in a dull, dragging tone. 'Yeah. I can hear you. Give me a little time. I just ran out of guts is all. Need a little time, is all.'

Jordan was standing there, his cold-reddened face encircled by the shawl over the top of his hat and knotted at his throat. It made his lean, ruddy features look fat.

His glance went to Harris and remained there. Paul Jordan was, like Jess, a man of practical hard-headedness. Also like Jess, he lacked tact. 'Can't do it,' he told Harris, and gestured with a coatsleeve covered with snow. 'It's coming down faster.'

Jess opened his eyes, half-protected by soggy hatbrim. 'Paul . . . ?'

Before Jordan could reply Harris stood up looking for the old rangerider. 'Travois,' he said. The wiry man came from the far side of his horse.

'By gawd, why didn't I think of that!'

Even Paul Jordan was captivated by the idea. But it required a full hour to break off two small saplings, lash them at both ends with lariats, wide in back, crossing over one another, then wide again at the top where they would be tied with more lass-rope to someone's saddle. Making cross-pieces of pine boughs was the simplest part.

They immediately encountered a formidable difficulty. Neither Jordan's mount nor the greener colt the wiry older man was riding would have anything to do with the travois.

Paul swore, got bucked off, swore some more and arose angry when Harris said, 'Take Garth, one of you.'

They shifted the dead man to the back of Jordan's horse, and this time when the horse tried to buck Paul rawhided him from one end to the other. The horse, like all horses, had just enough intelligence to know which was the lesser of two evils; they tied Garth down and

138

Paul swung into his saddle.

The ridgling stood while the travois-ends were roped to his saddle, turned to look back, to sombrely study the strange contraption behind him, and when Harris stepped up the ridgling leaned without a single false move and began dragging along, using his weight to move Jess upon the crude means of getting him down to the open country.

Paul shook his head while eyeing the ridgling. He had never liked the seal-brown. No one else had ever liked him, for that matter, except his owner. Jordan faced forward and rubbed numb hands together as he led off again.

The snow had a little occasional gust of icy wind to it now, swirling flakes up under hatbrims into cold faces and wet eyes.

Jordan rode the trail another mile, asked how the ridgling was coming along, and when Harris said he couldn't do better, Paul turned off the trail, down-slope. They could have had difficulty here except that Jess's solid weight forced travois-pole-ends deep into the snow, holding the conveyance back. It did not run up onto the ridgling the way something with wheels would have done, and the drifts were deeper now, making it easier for the horses to remain upright. Paul did not look back again for a half hour, until they were skirting through thinner stands of trees with stumps showing above the snow. Down here was where Jordan's outfit had been making winter-wood for many years; there was less interference from standing timber.

The snow-covered grassland came up into the foothills. Jordan halted when they came out of the final stand of big timber, looked back, wagged his head at the plodding ridgling, and turned eastward out through the broken country of the foothills heading toward the place he had told Galt to meet them. His wiry rider cackled with relief when they were back in lower country. 'We don't need no wagon,' he said. Maybe he was right. Maybe they could have reached the ranch with Jess on the travois. One thing was sure, they could easily reach the red rock territory where Galt was to meet them, and with plenty of time to make a fire, something they all needed.

Gusts of wind came more often, but down in the foothills, protected often by little knobs and upthrusting hillocks, it was easier to avoid the worst of the wind.

They reached the place of rendezvous with the wagon, which to Harris Bolton looked exactly like every other mile of this dismal, bitterly cold countryside, but which evidently looked different to Paul Jordan and his hired rider. Jordan halted, leaned to dismount as though both legs were frozen, and made a face when his feet touched down. 'Wood,' he said, through grey lips, and stumped back where Jess was lashed to the travois.

The rangerider scuttled for something that would burn. Harris too went back to look at his brother. Jess had snow over him and on his face. They brushed some of it off and he looked up at them from eyes that were nearly closed and hidden by his hatbrim. 'I don't think I'll go ridin' with you fellers any more,' he said.

Harris and Jordan cracked cold faces in smiles of relief. Paul leaned down so the wind would not whip his words away. 'The In'ians rode these things, Jess. You'd ought to be able to.'

'The In'ians—can damned well have 'em, Paul. You got any of that whisky left?'

Jordan trudged back to his patient-standing horse.

CHAPTER FOURTEEN

THE RANCH

The fire smoked and hissed, the wind occasionally whipped around into their protected place making them fan at smoke and cough, but the heat was worth it.

Howard, the wiry old rangeman, rubbed snow on Jess's face and hands; massaged it in hard, then dried his face and roughly jerked the travois around so Jess was facing the fire.

They finished that bottle; it helped for a while

to kindle body heat, and Harris surmised that—with any luck—by the time physical depletion set in among them, Galt had ought to be out here with the wagon.

It was a good guess. Galt returned with considerable noise and cursing, his massive harness-horses bucking drifts almost three feet high, their breath like smoke in the bitter cold.

He had brought back three blankets, beneath the wagon-seat to keep them dry, and they boosted Jess up, in atop the soggy straw, wrapped him like a mummy, and started for the ranch with that gusting wind swooping down to buffet them repeatedly once they got clear of the foothills.

Galt leaned from the high seat to yell something to his employer. Jordan had to get next to the fore-wheel to hear it.

'Fred's not back from town!'

Jordan nodded and veered off. It did not matter whether his rangeboss got back tonight or not. He could have used him back up yonder; in fact he leaned heavily upon Fred Baker, but they had managed well enough by themselves.

The storm got in behind them. Horses plugged along, heads down, backs humped, tails flattened against rumps. The men braced against gusts of wind and Galt, up on his wagon-seat, abruptly veered, then whistled, and through the snowfall it was finally possible to make out a steadily-glowing little bunkhouse window.

They did not dismount at the tie-rack in front of the barn, but followed the wagon on inside. Finally, the wind was thwarted.

They carried Jess into the lighted bunkhouse, then Galt and the wiry older man went back to care for the livestock, to stall them, fork down big baits of hay, and pitch a little grain into the feed boxes.

Jordan helped Harris get his brother settled upon a lower bunk before going over to stoke up the woodstove, make sparks fly when he poked in fresh burls from the scuttle along the back-wall. Then Paul stood over there, icy water dripping to the floor, his coat beginning to steam, and not until his riders returned did he shed his hat, his gloves, shawl and coat.

Without speaking he went to the bunkhouse cupboard and returned with several tins and a fry-pan, and went to work to prepare a meal.

The heat was more than a blessing to nearly-frozen men, it was the only thing which could preserve them. Howard kept grinning and the younger rangeman, Galt, sat down to shed soggy, stiff boots, and to roll and light a smoke. He rubbed his cheeks and watched Paul Jordan arranging cooking pans atop the wood-stove, then arose to dig out tin plates and cups to set upon the table.

Outside, the storm seemed to occasionally fade down to nothing more malevolent than steady snowfall. Then the wind would return. Once, Howard cocked his head, bird-like, then swore.

Jess gradually loosened all over. Harris peeled him down to shirt and boots and britches, draped Jess's gunbelt from a wall-peg, capped it with his brother's disreputable filthy old hat, and was the last among them to shed his own half-frozen outer garments. Then he went over and drank deeply from the water-bucket, which prompted Howard to say, 'I'd say the last thing any of us would need for a spell would be more wetness.'

Jordan turned. 'Howard, did you grain the ridgling?'

The older rider cackled. 'Half again as much as the other horses. You figure he deserved it?'

Jordan gazed at Howard, 'Don't you figure he earned it?'

'Hell yes. And then some. If that mean bastard belonged to me he'd spend the rest of his life just wanderin' around a big pasture eatin' and not havin' to do another blessed thing.'

Jordan worked at the wood-stove. It was not a cook-stove but it had been used by many riders over the years as one. Paul Jordan was unmarried and had never grown large enough to build a cook-shack and hire a cook. He and his men had been living off the top of that stove a long while, and none of them seemed the worse for it.

Over at the main-house Jordan had another bottle of whisky and as he was ladling up their meal at the table he sent Galt over there.

When the cowboy returned he was wet above the knees, and cold. Backing to the fire after placing the bottle atop the table he said, 'This here isn't just the first storm of the year, but all the others are goin' to have to strain some to equal it.'

Jess was asleep when they went over to feed him, so they let him sleep and returned to their own meal. Paul drank scalding coffee and said, 'He isn't goin' to be in any shape to winter-feed, Harris. Maybe not for a month.'

There was no argument there. 'I'll take time off from lawing in town,' the sheriff replied between mouthfuls. He was more ravenous than he had thought.

Jordan hadn't said that to get this kind of response. 'Howard can take a couple of horses and bunk at Jess's place and do the chores.'

The wiry rider bobbed his head, perfectly agreeable.

'You need your men here,' stated Harris, and Jordan shook his head.

'Naw. Two of us can feed, and until some of this snow melts nobody can ride out anyway. I can spare Howard easy.'

Harris accepted for his brother. 'We're right obliged, Paul.'

'Well,' stated Jordan, arising to re-fill his cup, 'I had a stake in that bear. He cost me a good old cow and he sure as hell would have cost me more. Maybe a rider. Maybe some horses, to boot.' He returned to the table and set the coffeepot down. 'About that Crippen killing. How did he get close enough to catch the horse with Tom on his back?'

Harris could not answer that. All he could do was recite what he had been told, and what he and Jess had guessed after visiting the place where the killings had occurred, and also what they had thought about the bear, after their encounter with him. He was sure it would not sound very convincing to rangemen who knew horses, and at least to some extent, knew bears.

But not a single word of doubt was uttered. In fact Galt added something to it. 'Out in the open with a clear path, and bein' as big as a horse— bigger, by gawd—I'd say that son of a bitch could just about out-run a horse.'

But the grizzly had not done that. Harris and Jess knew he hadn't; they had seen the place where the attack had taken place before the storm. There had been no evidence of a race. But—he did not speak, he concentrated on eating. It would have done nothing but help the legend of a grizzly bear as cunning, as sagacious as a human being, to recount what Harris thought—what he *knew*. All he eventually said was: 'One way or another that bear had to be done away with.'

Paul pushed back his plate, scratched and gazed over at Jess, sleeping like a log, warm and totally relaxed. 'Wish there was a doctor in Canbyville,' he mumbled.

Howard grinned. 'Busted ribs and a wrenched back is all, Paul. I seen 'em like that two dozen times in my lifetime. But there's one damned sure thing: He'll get over it in time, and he's big an' young an' stout as a bull, but wait— give him another ten, fifteen years and he'll know it's still there. Rheumatics settle in them places in a feller. It don't show up for a long while, but eventually it does. Me; fifteen years back a gawddamned drunk idiot in Nevada stumbled out'n a saloon at Tonopah shootin' off his pistol. I was across the road tyin' my horse at a rail, and a bullet caught me ahind the right knee . . . I was three months gettin' over that . . . Three winters back it come back on me.' Howard shoved his plate away. 'Now, I wish I'd shot that crazy bastard.'

Howard waited. When the others had no comment to offer he also said, 'Maybe, all the same, Harris, it wouldn't do no harm to load him on a stage and take him south where they got some doctors.'

A high gust of wind rattled cedar shakes atop the bunkhouse roof and made the one window in the log structure quiver, then it soughed away southward swirling up blinding clouds of fallen

147

snow.

Jordan went to peer out and wag his head before going back to the table to make some Irish coffee with the whisky. There were going to be some humped-up cattle come morning, and some damned deep drifts, but generally, when the wind accompanied one of these snowstorms out in open range country, it also blew the snow off the frozen grass.

Jess did not awaken for an hour. Harris was sitting flush-faced and stocking-footed, asleep in a tipped back chair when Galt came over and shook him. Galt jerked a thumb and Harris came up to his feet with a solid fear. But all Galt had meant was that Harris's brother was awake.

He looked up, looked past, looked around the hot little snug room where two men were snoring, Howard and Paul Jordan, lying out fully clothed atop bunks, and looked up again. 'How did I get here?'

Harris got some stew in a tin cup and leaned to feed Jess. 'On an Indian sled out of the mountains, in Paul's feed-wagon the rest of the way. I'll shove this stew into you, and you swallow. How do you feel?'

'Like a herd of razorbacks ran over me and the last one kicked. You got any drinkin' water in here?'

Harris got a dipperful and had to do that twice before his brother's thirst was slackened. Then he spooned stew into Jess, until his

148

brother cursed and struggled to hoist himself into half a sitting position so he could feed himself. As he ate he listened to the storm. Between mouthfuls he said, 'Those In'ians was right after all,' and showed Harris a rueful smile. When he finished eating he lay back breathing shallowly. 'I got aches where I didn't even know a man had places to ache.'

Howard came over, grinning, his little shrewd eyes intent. 'You need your ribs bandaged,' he told Jess Bolton. 'They won't heal straight an' all if you just let 'em go. Want me to do it?'

Jess, who knew the Jordan rider from the past riding season, cocked an eye as he said, 'You sure you know how, Howard?'

The wiry cowboy snorted. 'I've done it more times than I can shake a stick at. If you've been in as many bunkhouses as I've been in, Jess, you know how easy it is for fellers ridin' green horses to get busted rib-bones. Sure I can do it. But we got to have some strips of cloth.'

Neither Paul Jordan nor the younger cowboy, Galt, awakened as Harris and Howard rummaged for something to make bandages out of. Harris found an old muslin sheet and Howard fastened onto it with sounds of exultation. He ripped the sheet, tested it for strength and told Harris to strip his brother to the waist.

For Jess, Howard's swift, confident moves were difficult to bear. Howard did in fact know what he was doing, but he had never bothered to learn any gentle ways to do it.

It helped, though. Jess was lying there sweating and sipping whiskyed coffee, testing his ability to breathe, and without smiling said, 'It don't hurt quite as much any more.'

Howard was rolling a smoke and raised shrewd eyes in a grin. 'I think you got a hurt back too, Jess. There's nothin' to be done about that, except you got to stay off rough horses, don't lift nothin' and sleep on some planks for a month or two.'

Jess scowled at Howard. 'How do I do all that when I got cattle and horses to winter-feed?'

'That's been took care of,' replied the wiry older man, licking cigarette paper, folding it over and popping the finished product between his lips. He turned to go after something to light up with and did not explain, so Harris did, and Jess gazed after Howard as he listened to his brother, then shook his head. But whatever that meant he did not explain. He felt his sore rib-cage, tenderly, considered his brother and winked.

Harris winked back.

The wind was dying, which may have had some significance. But when Harris went to the window to look out, the snowfall was as heavy, perhaps even a little heavier, than it had been.

He leaned there looking at mounded white rooftops around the ranch-yard, waited for the wind to return, and when it didn't he craned upward to see the sky beyond the little overhang-roof of the bunkhouse. The only thing to be seen was snowfall.

He straightened up, looked around, saw that even Howard was now stretched out upon a bunk, and went in search of a place to also sleep.

Not until he was off his feet in the warmth and security of the sturdy log bunkhouse did his own series of aches manifest themselves. He smiled and closed his eyes. Regardless of the abuse his body had taken over the past twenty-four hours, all that was now over with, finished, and behind him.

CHAPTER FIFTEEN

PEOPLE

In the morning there was blinding sunlight. No warmth but eye-stinging brilliance.

Harris joined Paul Jordan on the little bunkhouse porch to survey their white, virgin world. The sky was blue and flawless. How that storm had managed to dissipate during the few hours they had been asleep inside was a mystery, but it had; even those lingering shards of soiled storm-clouds which commonly littered a storm-swept sky were absent.

Drifts were in some places eave-high among the ranch structures. In other places the wind had scoured the earth right down to the tawny grass.

Paul Jordan gazed off in the direction of town. 'You're welcome to leave Jess here,' he said. 'But if you'd feel better having him in town you're welcome to take my light buggy. We can fix up something for him to lie on, and it looks like the way's clear. You can go around any big drifts but it don't seem likely you'll see many.' He turned toward the storm-hazed high mountains northward, and shook his head as he dropped a cigarette into the snow beside the building. 'I wish to hell I'd measured that bear.'

Galt and Howard came back from forking feed to the horses, hats tipped to shield eyes which could not be protected from sunlight bouncing upwards from the snow.

Jess seemed better this morning. At least he ate like a horse and Howard cackled that this was a certain sign of recovery.

When they got him settled in Jordan's light rig, with the buffalo rifle, his bridle and saddle, and tied the ridgling on one side of the tailgate, Jess smiled and waved as the sheriff struck out. He was wrapped with three blankets and bundled with someone's ancient, sweat-smelly shawl. His general appearance was evil; he was wearing filthy clothing, his hat had mountain-mud ingrained in the felt, he was unshaven and

152

sunken-eyed, but when Harris turned to look back, Jess grinned and accused him of knowing where every chuck-hole lay beneath the snow.

They talked very little. Around them an utterly still, empty and silent world inhibited conversation. As far as they could see there was nothing but whiteness, miles on end of it. Behind, where the Jordan ranch lay in a gentle swale, only one rooftop showed and it was mounded with four inches of snow.

The sun brightly shone. There should have been more warmth than there was, but neither of the Boltons were especially troubled. For one thing their shrunken guts had had the pleats taken out by a supper last night and a breakfast this morning. That is all animals—two-legged or otherwise—require to be capable of generating bodyheat.

And each of them had his private thoughts. Gradually, all that had happened came back to Jess. There were blank spaces but he remembered most of it, and once, while they were mid-way with nothing to fix their course on, he said, 'I wish I'd fetched back one of the casings from the buffler gun.'

Harris, leaning forward, driving with slack lines, turned his head. 'You got enough to remember that bear by.'

'Naw. For the little girl. For Farnham's little girl.'

Harris straightened forward. Maybe, a little

153

boy would have treasured something like a bullet casing from the men who had killed the grizzly bear which had killed his grandfather, but it did not seem to him that a little *girl* would want anything like that.

'An ear,' Jess said. 'An ear an' a casing.'

Harris leaned back, shucked his gloves and felt for his tobacco sack. 'It's a litle *girl*, Jess.'

For a while Jess rode along in silence, then he too felt for a tobacco sack as he said, 'What'll they do with Sam Garth, back at Jordan's place?'

'Bury him I suppose. When the ground thaws out enough. I got no idea what else they could do with him.'

Harris caught a brief flash of distant light and stopped building his smoke to watch for it again. Then he lit up and sighed. There were several of them; sunlight bouncing back off the windows in town. He sat there allowing the ranch horse to pick its own route and gait. 'I never thought Canbyville was a pretty place. Did you, Jess?'

'No. Is it?'

'Yeah. Like one of those pictures on the calendars horseshoe companies send out at Christmas time. Snow on the rooftops, smoke risin' and all.'

Jess lit up in the wagon-bed, almost coughed, and a spasm of searing pain went through his chest from the near-cough. He raised his arm and dropped the smoke outside the wagon.

'Where do you figure to put me up, if I can't go home? The jailhouse?'

Harris looked around. 'The rent's free.'

'And the food's terrible,' grumbled Jess.

'Up at the boardinghouse. They have an empty room next to mine. Jess; you want to rest up a few days then go hunt up a doctor?'

'No. What for? Pay a pill-roller a couple of dollars to tell me I got some broken ribs and maybe a sprained back.'

The horse evidently knew exactly where the liverybarn was, because without urging he trailed off to his right to enter the back alley on the west side of town. They drove up out back before Harris picked up the lines and turned in the opposite direction. The only thing wrong with the horse's notion was that he did not realise they had to first unload Jess at the boardinghouse up at the other end of Canbyville.

The liveryman came out back, watched, scratched his head as he recognised the ridgling on the tailgate, then stood back there until he knew where the rig was going. Then he went back inside, up through and out front, scuffing soiled roadway snow on his hurrying way to the general store, and after that to the saloon.

There were two snowed-in freighters at the boardinghouse who aided Harris in getting his brother into the room and atop the bed. They were interested in what had happened and all Harris told them was that his brother had fallen across a deadfall pine the day before. They accepted it.

When Harris returned to the liverybarn by way of the same back-alley he evidently was not seen until he got down there and whistled up the dayman to hand the horses and rig over, with instructions, because no one came looking down there for him.

Afterwards, he went up to the jailhouse. It was habit; he had no prisoners—hadn't had any since the riding season had ended—and the letters which had been shoved under the door by the store-clerk from across the road did not look any different from the other letters he usually received. He threw them atop the desk, felt the cold in here, debated about making a fire and finally decided on just a small one. Maybe he would return today and maybe not.

Out front, he got a surprise. That pudgy medical practitioner who had examined Old Man Farnham and had cared for his surviving granddaughter, was coming toward the jailhouse from the direction of the general store. Behind him northward up the roadway someone waved. It was John Southwick out front of his saloon. Harris waved back, then stepped aside for the doctor to enter, but he stopped at the door looking up.

'I got back to town last night to look in on the

child. Sooner than I expected, Sheriff, but that's the way things go sometimes.' Doctor Ray sniffed, ran a mittened hand under his nose and then said, 'There were some conflicting rumours around town last night, Sheriff. One was that you went after a gigantic grizzly bear, and the other one was that a man named Jordan's hired riders killed the bear which injured the Farnham child and killed her grandfather.' Doctor Ray cocked his head. 'I'd say from your appearance, Sheriff, that you went after the grizzly.'

If Harris was supposed to admit where he had been and what he had done up there, it was the wrong approach. He said, 'I'm glad you're back in town. My brother's up at the boardinghouse with some bandaged ribs and maybe something wrong with his back. I'd sure take it kindly, Doctor, if you'd go up there and look him over.' Harris stepped down and smiled. 'I got to go over to the bath-house.' He nodded and walked away.

The snow underfoot was melting. It no longer had that crisp, squeaky sound when a man walked upon it. Now, his boot went completely through and slushy icewater rose up around his foot. But that increasing mid-day warmth was welcome. People came forth to shop and talk and perform tasks they had abandoned the day before when the storm had been clearly on its way.

But not everyone was entirely convinced it was warm enough for bathing, yet, so Harris Bolton had the bath-house to himself. One grimy window facing the west caught some sunlight and reflected it inward. Otherwise, there was the barrel-stove which heated bathwater and the little house simultaneously, and Harris had to fire that stove up before he got near the dented old tin tub.

It was an ordeal, but a worthwhile one when he could finally lie back soaking. As he had finally been able to do last night at Paul Jordan's bunkhouse, he now thought back, considered events and circumstances. Privately he derived satisfaction from his own behaviour, and from the conduct of his brother. They had not reacted identically in each interlude but they had both acted consistently with their characters and their personalities, which was the only real way to make judgments about people.

When he climbed out to towel off the bath-house was hot, the window was steamy, and when Harris finally departed he left the door open.

He had to shave out back of the boardinghouse where his shaving things were, and after completing that job too, he felt about normal again.

Jess was lying gazing out the closed window of his little room at the southward view directly down the south roadway when Harris walked in.

Jess glanced up. 'You look a sight better,' he said and smiled to indicate the fresh and professional bandage around his upper body. 'That's the first doctor I ever run across that had common sense. He had a pony of whisky inside his coat and each time I'd groan, he'd rear back and hand me the bottle. Then he'd take a swallow too.'

Harris's eyes twinkled as he pulled around a chair to sit on. 'What did he say?'

'That I owe him a dollar for a house call.'

'What else?'

'Two busted ribs, three cracked ones an' a dislocated vertebra, which he punched back into shape, and I damned near went right up through the ceiling when he did it.'

'Anything else?'

'No. You were figurin' there might be something else?'

Harris shook his head. 'I plain didn't know. How do you feel?'

'Half drunk and pretty damned good, Harris. Best I've felt in some days, I can tell you.' Jess smiled. 'He's comin' back in the morning to look me over. For another dollar. They're sure money-hungry bastards, aren't they? But with this one I don't mind at all.'

'You want a bath and a shave?'

Jess considered. 'Well, tomorrow I can shave myself. He said I can walk a little startin' tomorrow. But that bath—there's snow on the

159

ground, Harris. Do you remember old Walt Dunninger who took a bath this time of year when we were kids and caught the pneumonia and was dead the next month?'

Harris arose. He had something else to do before suppertime. 'I'll be back directly with some grub from the cafe.' He considered his brother. 'It'll be all over town. Did you tell the doctor?'

'Yeah. He asked how I got hurt and I told him all of it.'

'About Sam Garth too?'

'Yeah. He was part of it, wasn't he—the horse stealin' son of a bitch.'

Harris nodded, not over what his brother had said but over his opinion concerning what would happen now. He and his brother would have to tell and re-tell the story of their bear-hunt from now on. Well hell, it was something he would just as soon not have to continually talk about, but on the other hand they were both at least alive to tell it, and that was more important.

He left Jess with his euphoric feeling, returned to the roadway with shadows forming far out as the afternoon waned, and struck out down in the direction of the blacksmith shop.

John Southwick saw him across the road from the saloon and called over. 'Got some warm toddy in here, Sheriff, when you get round to it.'

Harris threw John a genial wave and kept on

160

walking.

There were rivulets of icewater along each side of the road, vehicles and hooves had ground the snow into whitish mud by now, stovepipe smoke hung in the late-day, still air, and there was a hint of oncoming cold again for tonight, and when the sheriff crossed over and turned for a moment to glance back northward up through town, he saw snow-clouds like smoke hanging above the far-away mountains where the scarlet sun was settling lower by the moment.

For one vivid moment he again saw that huge bear blinking, blinded by muzzleblast-brilliance. He could recall the sour, foetid, boar-bear scent, then he turned and went down the alley to the little house with the immaculate solitary front window.

Eleanor Farnham opened the door to him. Without a word she stepped aside, and smiled as he came inside. The small parlour was pleasantly warm. There was a wonderful aroma of cooking, and as he removed his hat and turned to ask about Cindy, Eleanor held out a hand for the hat. He let her take it, watched her turn to hang it from a wall-peg, and when she faced him again there was not even a hint of that dullness he had last seen in her gaze.

She said, 'Word travels fast, Harris . . . I have coffee in the kitchen.'

He followed her out there and took the chair she pointed to, then watched her fill two cups at the stove. She was a tall woman, wide-shouldered, long-legged, strong in the back and arms. Without turning she said, 'They say you found him and killed him.' When she faced around he was gently shaking his head. She brought over the cups and sat opposite him. 'I told you—word travels fast.'

'But I didn't tell anyone.' He reached for the cup under her steady gaze, and lifted it. 'Yeah, that's what happened. My brother and I. It took a little doing.' He tasted the coffee. It was strong and pleasant, not reboiled this time. He leaned back. 'How's Cindy?'

'Better. In a minute we'll go see her.' Eleanor lowered her eyes to the cup she was cupping in both hands. 'We heard in town about that young cowboy the bear killed.'

'Tom Crippen.'

'Do you know how that happened?'

'No, ma'am, and I doubt if we'll ever know. That wasn't an ordinary bear, Eleanor.'

'Was he very large?'

Harris sighed under his breath. 'Yes. Cindy sized him up about right. He was the biggest bear I'd ever seen. Bigger than one of Paul Jordan's upgraded bulls.'

'And your brother?'

'He's up at the boardinghouse resting. He got some busted ribs but he'll be all right. That doctor's in town, Eleanor.'

'Yes, I know.' She raised her eyes to him

162

again. 'He was here a little while ago.'

Harris nodded. *That* was where she had heard about the bear-kill. But it didn't matter, not really; there was not going to be any way to be reticent about what had happened and he might just as well become reconciled to that.

Eleanor said, 'Cindy asked where you were. The doctor told her you and your brother had gone into the mountains and had killed the bear ... Harris; she wants to see you ... That buggy-ride you mentioned?'

He nodded. 'Sure. As soon as she's able. Maybe on the first warm day. A picnic...?'

Eleanor did not lower her eyes. 'She'd be so happy.'

He felt colour coming when he said, 'If you'd come along, Eleanor,' and reached again for the coffee cup.

She arose without looking at him. 'I'd love to.'

They went to her daughter's tiny bedroom. Cindy's large eyes came up in a wondering sweep when Harris filled the doorway. The dark rings were still there, but not as noticeable now as they had been a few days ago. He eased down upon the side of the bed and took a small hand into his own hand. 'You sure look pretty,' he told the child, and winked at her.

She furiously blushed. 'I'm glad you're back, Uncle Harris. I—was scairt when the doctor told me where you'd gone.'

163

'Well, maybe someday we'll talk about that, but right now we got to plan that buggy-ride with your maw and a picnic basket.'

Her small hand was warm in his palm, soft and strangely wonderful. 'In the snow?' she said.

'No. But the sun'll hang around for a while maybe, and when the snow goes off and it's warm out, and you're able to ride out.'

'Would you have supper with us, Uncle Harris?'

He did not know what to say. He looked up. Her mother, arms folded across her chest, was looking steadily at him. She nodded, smiling gently with her mouth and eyes. He said, 'I'd like that, Cindy. We can maybe sit in here and have supper and talk.' He placed her hand atop the quilt and arose.

She said, 'Will you wash my face?'

That stopped him in his tracks too, but her mother eased over the moment by saying, 'In a minute, Cindy,' and led the way out of the room. He was in the doorway when the child looked up and said, 'Uncle Harris?' When he turned she soberly winked at him. He winked back.

In the kitchen Eleanor looked close to laughing. He had not seen her like that in several years. She looked young and very handsome, the way he remembered seeing her for the first time. 'Sheriff, you're not used to little girls.'

He sank down in the chair at the table again. 'No. That's a plumb fact, I'm not.' He looked at the cups. 'I—I can't explain it, Eleanor. She's so little in some ways and so . . .'

'Wise and innocent, Sheriff, and trusting—and hopeful. That's what little girls are . . . Do you like hamhocks and beans?'

He looked up again. 'Yes'm.'

She went to the stove. 'I didn't want her to find another person to put her faith in so soon, Sheriff. She loved her grandfather with her whole heart. He was older—it was not so hard for him to live up to her expectations.'

Harris waited for her to say more but she got busy with the oven. He thought he understood what she was saying, but again, he had no answer. This was an environment he had never experienced before and had not even suspected might exist. Being a single man on into his prime years had left him ignorant of some things, many things in fact.

He sat in sombre thought until she came over to re-fill the coffee cup, and glanced up at her. She was different; she had smiled and she had almost laughed. She even *looked* different. When their eyes met she said, 'If she hadn't needed someone so badly right now. More than a mother, Sheriff.'

He blurted it out. 'Well hell, Eleanor, that don't have to be a one-way street does it?'

She put down the pot. 'Harris, did you ever own a puppy that shagged you around and constantly watched you, and did not believe there was another human being like you in the world?'

'Sure,' he said.

'Then multiply all that by ten, or a hundred, and you'll have some idea what it's like to have a little girl worshipping you ... Harris, you've never had a family.'

He continued to gaze at her. 'That don't mean I can't have one, Eleanor ... I think those beans are burning.'

She turned swiftly toward the stove. He sat gazing at her, beginning to wonder about something he had never really seriously thought about before, and it was strangely, almost painfully, pleasant to consider it.

Photoset, printed and bound in Great Britain by REDWOOD BURN LIMITED, Trowbridge, Wiltshire